MASTER OF MAGIC

DRAGON'S GIFT THE VALKYRIE BOOK 5

LINSEY HALL

For my dear friend Eleonora.

1

As our monster truck raced through the forest, joy surged through me. I stood on the fight platform at the front, clinging to the rail as the truck swerved around giant trees, driven by my sister Ana.

For the first time in five years, I was fighting monsters with *both* my sisters.

I looked over at Rowan, grinning so hard my cheeks hurt.

After five long years of searching, we'd finally found her. Saved her. Two days ago, I'd yanked her from the grips of the Rebel Gods, and now the three of us were back together. Me, Ana, Rowan.

A team.

And right now, our job was to catch the giant cryptid that was haunting this ancient Scottish forest.

"See anything up ahead?" Ana called from behind the wheel.

"Just trees!" I shouted. "No Nessie yet."

"Are we sure this is Nessie?" Rowan asked. Wind whipped her hair back from her eager face. "The legs—not to mention being on *land*—seem seriously out of character."

I laughed. She was right. Nessie with legs was weird.

"According to Jude, someone had hit her with an evolution charm. She'd grown legs and charged up here, to the Ancient Forest."

I was glad this little side job for the Protectorate had come up. Rowan had been a captive too long, and this gave her a chance to get back into the real world. Doing what we'd always done best —practice our general badassery from our perches on the buggy.

I patted the bag of potion bombs slung over my shoulder, nodding to the identical one hanging off of Rowan's back. "These potion bombs should tranq her. Then the Cryptos will take over and get her back to normal."

"And stick her back in Loch Ness, I hope," Rowan said. She'd always loved animals.

"Yep." I grinned at her, clinging hard to the rail as Ana swerved the vehicle around a huge tree. "The Protectorate wouldn't have it any other way. They work for good, Rowan. You'll like it here."

"I trust you, but—"

A blast of flame exploded from the trees to our left.

A scream caught in my throat as Ana swerved the buggy away, throwing out her hand and creating a white shield between us and the flame. The brilliant orange fire crashed against it, the heat warming my face.

As it faded, I caught sight of giant, gleaming green eyes peering out at me from between the charred tree trunks.

"Nessie shoots fire?" Rowan shouted.

"Evolution is amazing." I cackled. "Charge her, Ana!"

Rowan dug into her potion sack and withdrew a gleaming blue glass ball that Hedy had made for us. It was the size of a softball—fairly large for a potion bomb. "How many do we have to hit her with?"

"At least eight."

Rowan grinned. "All right, then. Twenty bucks I hit her with more!"

A grin stretched across my face, my heart feeling like it was filling with sparkling light. I was so damned happy to be back with Rowan that I didn't care if she won.

Didn't mean I wasn't going to try, though.

"You're on." I dug into my sack and withdrew one of the potion bombs.

The buggy bounced over roots and rocks as Ana careened around a tree and headed for Nessie. The beast roared and took off into the forest.

"We're not going to hurt you!" Rowan shouted.

Nessie's footsteps pounded harder.

"She's a smart one," I said.

"There's nothing for you to eat in this forest," Rowan shouted. "Wouldn't you like a nice fish instead of some nasty rabbit or stag?"

Nessie roared again.

"Is she disagreeing with you?" I asked.

"No idea."

We reached a clearing, and Ana hit the gas. The buggy jumped forward, eating up the ground.

"We can't take her out here!" I shouted. "This clearing is enchanted with magic that prevents transporting!"

If Nessie went down here, they'd never be able to transport her back to Loch Ness.

"Got it!" Ana cried, and sped faster after Nessie, getting out of the clearing entirely.

Soon, I could see Nessie's massive green tail as she raced through the forest on sturdy legs. The trees towered over her, three times the size of normal oaks. This ancient forest wasn't far from the Protectorate castle, but this was the first time I'd seen it.

"I'm going to block her way." Rowan thrust out her free hand.

A moment passed. I waited for her magic to fill the air.

But nothing happened.

A grimace twisted her face.

Still nothing.

"Are you okay?" Worry twisted my insides. During her time with the Rebel Gods, they'd totally screwed with her magic. They'd given her new powers, but what about her old ones?

A bead of sweat dripped down Rowan's temple. The buggy lurched over a bump, and she stumbled.

She gasped. "It's still not there."

"No telekinesis at all?" It was the gift she'd been born with, and she'd been having trouble with it in the two days she'd been free.

"I'm trying to move the fallen logs, and...nothing."

"Do you have your new gifts?" Ana shouted from behind. "The ones from the Rebel Gods?"

"No." Her voice cracked. "Those disappeared when their enchantment broke. I thought it would just take a little time for my old magic to come back, but if it's not appearing right now... when I most need it..."

"Don't say it." I scowled at her.

"It never will." She sucked in a ragged breath, then determination set her brow.

Now *that* was the Rowan I recognized.

Nessie had gained some distance. She was *really* not a fan of being chased.

"We need to lure her to us!" Rowan turned back to Ana. "Steer us over to that big tree!"

Ana swerved the buggy toward the large tree with a low-hanging branch. As she neared it, Rowan stashed her potion bomb in her sack, then leapt into the air, grabbed the branch, and scrambled onto it.

"What the heck?" Ana shouted.

"I'll draw it to me! Herd Nessie toward me with the buggy!"

"That's dangerous as hell!" Ana shouted. "You could get barbecued!"

"Compared to the last five years, this is nothing."

And she was determined not to fail. I knew Rowan. Losing her magic would tear a hole in her. But she wouldn't stay down. *Nothing* could keep her down.

And as much as Ana was a worrier, that wouldn't help us get the job done. I loved her for caring, but I wanted to catch Nessie. And I wanted Rowan to be able to prove herself. Not to me. But to herself.

"I like how you think." I unfurled my wings and leapt into the air, avoiding branches as I flew above Rowan. "I'll attack from the sky."

Rowan grinned up at me, looking slightly crazy.

"You're both nuts!" Ana drove away, looping around to try to corner Nessie.

The morphed sea creature was off in the distance, crashing through the forest and upsetting the animals. From up here, I could see stags charging away from her, along with a herd of badgers.

Nessie was *definitely* upsetting the ecosystem.

Ana drove the buggy in a large loop, herding Nessie toward us. The monster occasionally turned back to blast fire at Ana, but my sister was too fast. She threw out her protective shield, stopping the flames before they could give her a new, crispier hairdo.

"She's nearly here!" I called down to Rowan.

She dug into her potion sack. I rubbed the smooth glass of

the potion bomb with my thumb as I waited. Nessie thundered closer, her green skin looking a bit dry and flaky. She needed to get back into Loch Ness. Whoever had transformed her hadn't done a great job.

Leaves fluttered from the trees as Nessie's footsteps rattled the earth. She was nearly under Rowan when I hurled my first potion bomb. Rowan followed suit, and the blue glass balls exploded against Nessie's hide.

Nessie didn't even pause. She was far too big for that tiny amount of sleeping potion to have an effect.

I dug into my pouch to withdraw another ball as Nessie raced faster through the forest. Rowan ran after her, jumping from tree limb to tree limb like Tarzan. I flew fast, darting around trees to get the perfect position.

I threw the next bomb, grinning when it shattered against Nessie's butt. Rowan's second bomb hit her on the back, and Nessie stumbled.

She roared, then turned and blasted fire up at Rowan.

Fear turned my blood to ice, but Rowan dodged just in time, fast and agile. Her hair smoked a bit, but the dark strands look mostly intact.

My next bomb exploded against Nessie's neck, and Rowan managed to hit her on the side. Nessie wobbled as she ran, slowing down.

"One more!" I shouted, digging into the pouch.

We hurled our bombs at the same time, hitting Nessie on the back. She crashed to the ground, skidding against the leaves.

"Woo!" Rowan leapt from the tree limb and loped over to Nessie's head.

I flew down to join her and landed lightly on my feet. I was really starting to get the hang of the flying.

Rowan's wide gaze followed my wings as I drew them back into my body. "You've come a seriously long way."

"It's weird, to be honest." All my new powers were still settling down inside of me, learning to play nicely as I figured out how to properly use them.

Rowan knelt by Nessie's head and petted her cheek. She had a smooth face and tiny fangs. Cute, actually.

I pressed my fingertip to the comms charm. "Emily? We've got Nessie. You can come get her."

"Great! Be right there," said Emily, the transporter mage.

"They really won't hurt her?" Rowan asked.

"Not a chance." But I could understand how Rowan might have some trust issues. After what she'd been through, it was no surprise. "They'll transport her back to the loch and transform her."

"Good." Rowan stood, her eyes cast in shadow.

I reached out and rubbed her shoulder, wishing I could do more for her. Ana pulled the buggy to a stop next to us, her gaze landing on the two of us. A smile stretched across her face, but I could see worry at the edges.

Rowan's missing magic was a serious problem. As was the issue of the Rebel Gods. We might have killed one of them, but the other two were still out there.

Still hunting us.

An hour later, we arrived back on the main lawn at the Protectorate. Emily had transported Nessie back to her loch, and then returned to bring the buggy and us back to the Protectorate. The midday sun gleamed overhead, making the glass windows in the castle sparkle like diamonds.

"How'd you feel about your first job?" Emily asked Rowan.

"Um, good." Rowan's face was entirely shuttered. Any openness or happiness she showed us was markedly absent when she was around others.

Emily smiled and nodded, but she seemed to get it and just waved, then turned and strode toward the castle. The dark-haired transporter mage was very perceptive.

"I can't believe we live here now." Rowan gazed across the lawn.

In the distance, Caro, Ali, and Haris practiced with weapons on the lawn. The Pugs of Destruction ran in circles around nothing, and the castle rose tall against the sky. All in all, it was an amazing place full of new friends. But to Rowan?

I wasn't sure if she could see that yet, or if she was still trapped inside her terrible memories.

"Do you like it?" Ana asked as she drove us toward the stables where the buggy was stored. "Living here, I mean. It's been a couple days since you arrived. Any change of heart?"

"I do like it." She frowned, and it was obvious that the transition was harder than we thought it would be. "But I should probably start practicing weapons with them." She pointed to Caro, Ali, and Haris. "Given the state of my magic, I mean."

"You'll get it back." I squeezed her hand, but worry weighted my heart. I had no idea where her magic had gone, and it seemed she didn't either.

"Yeah. I'll get it back." Determination shrouded her voice. "We're going to need it if we want to defeat the Rebel Gods."

"How's your memory doing?" I asked as Ana drove into the stable and parked.

We all climbed out of the buggy.

Rowan rubbed her head, frowning. "Still crap. I can feel the knowledge—it's in there. But accessing it is hard."

"The fog on your mind," Ana said. "Isn't that what you called it?"

"Yeah." She led the way out of the stable toward the castle.

"The enchantment was so heavy. But it feels like the memories have been slipping away. And it's only been two days that I've been free."

"You had them, and now they're gone?" Ana asked.

"Just hard to reach," she said. "I don't think they're gone entirely. It's like they're at the tip of my tongue. Or on the edge of my brain."

"It's the perfect protection for the Rebel Gods," I said. "Some kind of spell that makes you forget whatever you knew about them."

"You're right," Rowan said. "As soon as I left them, I thought I remembered more. Now, those memories are trapped."

Hedy had been unable to help us with a memory recovery charm. Melusine had been a bust, too. So had Aerdeca and Mordaca. We were running out of options.

"What we need is Arach," Ana said.

"But she hasn't shown herself to us." The dragon spirit who presided over the castle had been gone for weeks. I'd spent hours in her library, begging her to show up to help us with Rowan's memory.

I'd hoped that the mission today would get her feeling more like herself—maybe shake a few memories loose.

It didn't seem like it was working.

As we neared the castle, the sound of rock music filtered down from one of the high towers. Caro was no longer practicing on the lawn, so I had to assume it was coming from her room. She was the resident music expert here.

Mayhem, my winged friend, flew out through the castle doors, her ghostly form passing right through the wood. As usual, she had a ham gripped in her mouth. She must have finished her race around the yard with the other pugs, and dropped in on the kitchen for a snack. The ham didn't stop her from giving an excited yip as she circled us in the air.

Rowan laughed, and my heart lightened.

We might have the pressure of the Rebel Gods hanging over us, but Rowan was *back*. She was stressed about her missing magic, but she was also happy. Most of the time, at least.

I was going to take it. Hold tight to the good stuff.

Like Cade, whom I hadn't seen since last night at the Whisky and Warlock.

I stepped onto the stairs leading to the main doors, and shivered as magic rolled over my skin.

"Do you feel that?" Rowan asked.

"Yeah." I shoved open the heavy door. Magic slammed me in the face, a signature so strong that I gasped. "Arach."

"Speak of the devil," Ana said. "Just who we wanted to talk to."

"Arach?" Rowan asked. "You mean the dragon spirit you're obsessed with?"

"Exactly." I hurried into the main hall. "She's here. I wouldn't mistake that signature anywhere. Come on."

They followed me down the hall toward Arach's room. Sconces flickered yellow light as we passed.

"What's made her show up now?" Ana asked from behind.

"No idea." I pushed open the door to her room, nearly staggering at the feel of her immense power, and pulled up short when I saw Cade.

He grinned at me, looking handsome as ever with his dark hair and chiseled features. Richly scented smoke filled the room, twining around him. Next to him, a basin of blood gleamed in the light. Arach stood by the flickering fire, her shimmery white body blending with the smoke. She was in her human form, a lovely woman with a strange face that was almost reptilian. Her long, simple dress glowed like the rest of her, and she looked like she could disappear at any moment.

I shot Cade a look that very clearly said, "What are you doing here?"

But it was Arach who answered. "Your friend here seemed very determined to call me to this realm." Her quiet voice resonated with power, shaking my bones. I'd be afraid if I hadn't met her before.

"How did he do that?" She'd come to me in the past when I'd called to her. Why not now? And why to Cade?

"I was in deep slumber. It takes great magic to wake me." She looked at Cade, then at the basin of blood. "He managed it."

I glanced at him.

The corner of his mouth quirked up. "It seemed important to you."

"No kidding." I wanted to hug him. Why hadn't he told me he was doing this? The basin of blood caught my eye, then the thin wound at his wrist.

Bingo.

That was why he hadn't mentioned it. I'd have wanted to take over and donate my blood. No doubt he wouldn't have liked that.

Arach drifted toward us, her magic rolling over me in waves. Her keen gaze landed on Rowan. "You're our newest member, if I'm not mistaken?"

"Not officially, no," Rowan said. "I have no magic. Not anymore. So I don't see how I can join you."

Arach's gaze searched Rowan's, and she raised a hand, hovering it by Rowan's shoulder. "May I?"

Rowan glanced at me, and I nodded. *You can trust her.*

Rowan seemed to read my eyes, and she looked back at Arach. "Fine. Not every day I get to meet a dragon."

Arach's mouth crooked up at the corner, and she laid her hand on Rowan's shoulder. Her grin turned downward quickly, and her brow wrinkled.

"What is it?" Nerves echoed in Rowan's voice.

I felt them myself, every muscle in my body drawing tight with tension. Cade shifted closer to me and wrapped his hand around mine. Comfort surged through me, but not enough to drive away fear for my sister.

Nothing would ever drive that away.

"They've broken something inside of you." Sadness and concern echoed in Arach's voice, something I'd never heard from her before.

"I can't say that I'm surprised." Any fear in Rowan's voice was covered with wry humor. She had to be freaking out right now, but Rowan was never one to show fear.

"How do we fix it?" Ana demanded.

"I don't know," Arach said. "But it is important that you do."

Rowan's gaze turned serious. "Can you help me recover my memories? I know how to find the Rebel Gods, but the information is harder to access than I expected it to be."

"Shouldn't we focus on fixing you?" Ana asked.

"*This* will fix me. We need to get them. They are dangerous. To the world. To *us*." Shadows drifted across their eyes. "They're planning something big. I know it. I can *feel* it. Right at the edge of my mind."

"We'll find them, Rowan," I said. "I promise."

"Rowan is right," Arach said. "The Rebel Gods are the greatest threat right now. Rowan can work to recover her magic, but the most important thing is stopping the ones who are hunting you."

Rowan turned back to Arach. "So, can you help me remember?"

"I can certainly try." She drifted toward the chairs by the fireplace. "Come."

We followed her, taking seats around the flickering flames.

Ana, Cade, and I squished onto the couch, while Rowan and Arach took the two chairs.

I leaned against Cade, drawing strength from him. I was doing that more and more lately, but wasn't sure I wanted to examine the reason. It might even have to do with the *L-word*, but right now, I needed to be focused on Rowan, not myself.

Arach leaned toward Rowan, her expression searching. "What do you remember?"

"I'm not sure." Rowan frowned. Her dark hair gleamed in the firelight. "But I do know that Cocidius and Eris won't be in their godly realms. Not anymore."

"Agreed," Cade said. "We know where their realms are located now. It'd be too dangerous to stay there."

Rowan nodded. "I think they have another location. Some place I've been, but it was hard to get to. They're planning something big. And there are more of them."

"How many?" I asked.

Her brow creased. "I don't know."

"That's what I'll help you remember," Arach said.

"How?"

"Lean forward." Arach gestured with her hand.

Rowan did so, and Arach's chair levitated slightly to shift across the ground and move closer to Rowan. It stopped right in front her, and Arach leaned in, touching her shimmering white hand to Rowan's temple.

Rowan gasped, her whole form glowing slightly.

"I'm giving you a bit of my power," Arach said. "Trying to clear the blocks on your mind. Just focus."

Rowan nodded and closed her eyes. Tension pulled my skin tight as we waited. Rowan had said the Rebel Gods were planning something big, but even if she hadn't said that, I'd have guessed it.

Now we just had to hope that Arach could help Rowan remember.

The room was silent as Arach fed her magic to Rowan. It crackled on the air, feeling like bubbles against my skin. Even my own mind felt clearer. Like I might be able to access forgotten memories if I tried hard enough.

Briefly, I was tempted to think of my mother. But I focused on Rowan instead. Her brow creased as she searched her mind, intense concentration on her face.

Finally, she stiffened and gasped. "They've found a way to track Bree's magic."

I swallowed hard. "What?"

"A complex spell. I failed to capture you in the fae realm, but they found a way to track your new magic from the Norse gods." She paused, clearly trying to unravel the memories in her mind. "They aren't quite finished yet—something about the spell isn't complete—but soon, they'll be able to find you."

"And with her, us," Arach said.

"I don't have to stay here." The thought popped quickly out of my mouth.

"Don't be silly," Arach said. "You're part of the Protectorate."

"But you do need to bring the fight to them," Cade said. "Don't give them time to find you."

I couldn't agree more. "Do you know how long we have until they can find me?"

A deep furrow cut through Rowan's brow. "Um...a few days? A week? It's all foggy."

"Okay, we can work with that," I said.

"What do they want?" Ana asked.

"Our power. Worshippers. Misery on earth. I don't know how it all fits together, or what the final plan is. But it's based in those three things."

Ugh, great.

"Can you recall how many there are?" Cade asked. "And where they are?"

"There are at least a dozen," Rowan said. "They only needed the three to control me. Cocidius, Eris, and Chernobog. And they have a higher, more central godly realm. Not like the little ones that belong to each individual god. This one is bigger, and created with all their magic. It is remote, so it is safe. It's like their headquarters. Only gods are strong enough to enter it— and those who are given their permission."

"Like you?" I asked.

She drew in a ragged breath, her face pale. "I went once. But what did I do there?" Her brow creased. "I can't remember."

"There is a stronger block on your mind here," Arach said.

Rowan's breath came faster. She was clearly trying to force the memory free.

"Calm yourself." Arach's voice was soothing. "You may not remember. That is okay."

"How did you get there?" Cade asked. "That's the most important part."

I met his gaze and nodded. *We* could go. We might not be invited, but he was a god and I was a Dragon God. So that would allow us entrance.

Rowan licked her lips. "Um, through an underground place. It was dark, and deep. A man... A guide... You can find him at the darkest part of the world. In Darklane. Where the worst magic comes from. There is an entrance, and he can lead you. He's called the Gatekeeper."

"Twenty bucks it's dangerous," Ana said.

Rowan smiled, and a tiny spark of happiness flared in my chest.

"I do remember being scared. And tired. I went with Cocidius once, I think, but it's not easy to access their godly headquarters."

"Perhaps that's one reason only Cocidius, Eris, and Chernobog were with you," Ana said.

"Maybe." Rowan nodded. "That sounds right, actually. The others *can* leave. And they will, for the right cause. But they'll stay in their lair if given the choice. It takes great magic for them to leave and walk upon the earth. That's why they had the stronghold at Kart-hadasht. It was easier for them to go there, and they could bring their minions and give them orders to do their bidding on earth. It was much easier than bringing minions to their headquarters."

"Do you remember any other details about their lair, or the journey to reach it?" Cade asked.

She bit her lip. "Look for the matching symbols, in order of smallest to largest. Press them."

"That's a bit odd," I said.

She frowned. "I know. I have no idea what it means, but I think it's literal." She leaned back, face sad. "But that's all I remember."

Arach removed her hand and drew away. The glow faded from Rowan, who looked even more bummed without it.

"I'd hoped to remember more," she said.

"That's hugely helpful, though," I said. "Cade and I will go immediately to their headquarters. Do some recon."

"I want to go," Rowan said.

"Same," Ana said.

"You aren't gods," Arach said. "Not yet. You won't be allowed access. It will be difficult even for Cade and Bree."

"And you need to work on getting your magic back," I said to Rowan. I rubbed my chest, still remembering the terrible feeling of my own magic fading.

As if she felt the same thing, Rowan rubbed her own chest. "I do. Though I have no idea how."

"We'll try to help," Arach said. "The Protectorate has resources."

"Thank you." Rowan's gaze brightened. "But I want in on the big fight. When we finally go after the Rebel Gods, I want part of the action."

Determination blazed in her voice. I couldn't blame her. She wanted vengeance for the last five years.

So did I.

"I think it goes without saying that I want a piece of the action too." Ana grinned.

"I have a feeling that we're going to need everyone's help when it comes time to defeat them," Cade said. "But for now, we'll do recon."

Arach turned to me. "According to the notes that Jude and Hedy left for me here, you've advanced quickly through your training, Bree. Albeit in an unorthodox fashion."

"Thank you."

"When you finish this job and destroy the Rebel Gods, your training will be complete. You're about two years ahead of most trainees, but you're a special case."

"Ha. A special case. I've been told that before." I grinned at Ana and Rowan.

Arach cleared her throat.

My smile dropped. "I'm sorry."

"As I was saying, once you are done with this, you may advance to any division you like as a true member of the team. With a full salary."

"Wow, thank you." Happiness flared in my chest. *I'd almost made it.*

"You've earned it." Arach turned to my sisters. "And you will, too, when your power comes in."

"I hope so," Ana said.

"For now, my biggest concern is the Rebel Gods." Rowan had

a slightly haunted look about her, and it drew me back to the present.

It didn't matter that I'd almost completed my training. My sisters needed me. If we didn't defeat the Rebel Gods, my training wouldn't matter.

Nothing would matter, because we'd be dead.

2

An hour later, Cade and I set off for Magic's Bend. Ana and Rowan had gone to work on Rowan's magic, leaving Cade and I to start the recon.

Mayhem flew alongside us as we walked through the enchanted forest at the edge of the Protectorate grounds. She did circles around the trees, zipping up and down the trunks to fly through the new-growth leaves. The forest was vastly recovered from the damage last month, but it would only stay that way if we managed to defeat the Rebel Gods.

Worry tugged at me, and I glanced at Cade. "If they can find me using my magic, that means they can take out the Protectorate."

His face was set in serious lines. "Aye. If they have a dozen gods, they could level this place." He reached for my hand and gripped it in his stronger one. "But it won't come to that. We'll see to it."

I squeezed his hand, liking his assurance. This was my home now—I'd do whatever it took to protect it.

The clearing with the portals beckoned us, and we stepped up to the one that led to Magic's Bend. It glowed with white light. I stepped through, and the ether sucked me in, making my head spin. After a moment, it spat me out in the now-familiar alley in the Historic District.

I breathed shallowly, trying to avoid the smell of pee that permeated the alley after a weekend of partying.

"Drunks really favor this alley, huh?" I asked.

"Aye. Perhaps the Protectorate should have checked that before putting the portal in the party district."

"Hindsight, and all that."

Mayhem zipped right out into the street, disappearing as if she had business to attend to.

"No doubt off to find more ham," Cade said.

"I'd say that's a safe assumption." I followed her onto the street and hailed the nearest taxi.

A glittery purple car pulled to a halt, and we climbed into the back seat. It was covered in pink leather, and I was pretty sure this was the same cab we'd taken when we'd come here seeking Cass's help.

"Darklane, please," I said.

The pixie driver saluted, then pulled a U-ey right in the middle of the street, careening toward Darklane.

I gazed out at the view as we passed, enjoying the sight of the largest magical city in the world. It really was quite the place. Would the Rebel Gods attack it, as well?

I had to assume so. Eventually, at least. Their kind didn't stop at one tiny taste of power. They wanted it all.

Rowan, Ana, and I were just the beginning. The fuel for their evil deeds.

The cab stopped abruptly on the main street, right before the turn into Darklane.

The pixie turned around and grinned, popping bubblegum that matched her green hair. "And here we are! Not driving down that road. You understand, I'm sure."

"Aye, thanks." Cade handed her a twenty and climbed out.

I followed and headed down the street, then took a left onto the main road that cut through Darklane.

Like The Vaults back in Edinburgh, Darklane was where the dark magic practitioners lived. As soon as I stepped onto the cobblestone street in this older part of town, the light dimmed. It was as if the clouds were perpetually over the sun when you were in Darklane. True, we were nearing sunset. But it was even darker here than it should have been.

"So, Rowan said that the guide to the gods' headquarters is in the darkest part of Darklane. And I'm not sure where that is," I said. "I think we should stop by Aerdeca and Mordaca's place and ask them."

Cade nodded. "Aye, they're our only friends in Magic's Bend. Or in Darklane, at least."

Even if they weren't our friends, they were still our best bet. The FireSouls might live on the other side of town, but they stuck to the right side of the law. Aerdeca and Mordaca, on the other hand...

If it was creepy, they'd know about it.

We set off down the street toward their shop, the Apothecary's Jungle. Three-story Victorian buildings loomed on either side of the street, their once colorful paint now blackened by age and dark magic.

Eyes seemed to peer out of the windows, making my skin crawl. A form drifted out of one of the walls, and I dodged into the street.

I glared at the figure, a middle-aged man with a creepy smile and three eyes that blinked at different times. He wasn't a ghost, so I had no idea how he walked through walls.

"Hello, pretty lady." He waggled an oblong object at me. Was that a hot dog? "Would you like to buy some sausage?"

I gaped at him as he pointed up to a sign over his head. *Darklane's Finest Sausages.*

He waggled the sausage again, and it flopped in the air.

I stifled a chuckle. "Boy, that *is* tempting. But I'm afraid I'm going to have to turn you down right now. Maybe later, though." *Not.*

He opened his mouth—no doubt to convince me more—but I hurried down the street.

"Finest sausages!" he called after us.

"Darklane is weird," I said.

"You didn't want the hog dog he wobbled like a corpse's—"

A bat flew down from a light post, cutting him off.

I laughed. "I think I know where you were going with that, and no, I don't think I'll be returning."

We continued down the road in silence, passing a few more creepy shops that radiated dark magic. Nothing to compare with the three-eyed sausage man, of course, but I definitely preferred the Grassmarket in Edinburgh to Darklane.

The Apothecary's Jungle looked closed as we approached, the door shut and the curtains drawn. The sign hanging over the door fluttered in the breeze, and we climbed the stairs to the house that had once been purple or blue, from the look of the paint peeking through the grime.

Cade knocked.

A few moments later, heels clicked toward the door from the inside.

When Mordaca opened it, she was in full Elvira getup, her black bouffant at least eight inches high and her makeup so heavy that it looked like a mask. The black dress plunged low, revealing a serious amount of cleavage.

"Well, well, to what do we owe this pleasure?" she purred. Her gaze raked over Cade.

"We were hoping you could give us a bit of information," I said.

She grinned, ruby lips parting to reveal perfectly white teeth. "It'll cost you."

She really was fabulous, in the most old-school horror film kind of way.

"Doesn't everything?" I asked.

"But of course. What is it that you want to know?"

"Where is the darkest part of Darklane? Where the worst magic comes from?"

Her brows dropped low, and she gestured us inside. "Keep your voice down."

"Really?" I stepped inside.

"Of course," she hissed. "The darkest part of Darklane? Why the hell would you want to go there?"

"Even *we* don't go there." Aerdeca descended the stairs, her white satin pantsuit gleaming in the light of the chandelier. Her blonde hair fell like slick water around her face.

"We just need to find it. It's important."

"You'll die," Mordaca said.

"I don't know, I'm pretty tough."

"She is," Cade said. "You should see her in a fight."

I grinned at him.

"You can't outfight the Master of the Crypt," Mordaca said. "One touch and you're dead."

Master of the Crypt? Hopefully we wouldn't run into him in our pursuit of the Gatekeeper.

"And he can't be reasoned with," Aerdeca said.

"Not that we know much about it," Mordaca added.

Aerdeca nodded, and I studied her dark eyes, believing her. They *really* didn't like that place.

"We really don't have a choice," I said. "Where would we find it?"

Mordaca sighed. "If you insist. It's in the cemetery, of course. Cliché, I know. But you asked for the darkest place. And the magic there is unmistakable. It's at the end of the main road. Take a right at The Banshee's Revenge pub, go to the end of the lane, then left. Once you feel like you want to puke, you're almost there."

"That'll be two hundred dollars." Aerdeca held out a hand.

I scowled at them, digging into my pocket and hoping I'd brought enough cash.

Cade beat me to it, handing over two crisp bills. "That was quite a bargain."

Aerdeca took the money, grinning. "We like you. But since you'll probably die in there, feel free to empty your pockets so at least your friends get the last of your cash."

Mordaca laughed. "She has a point."

"We won't die," I said. "I've got too damned much to fight for to let some dude named the Master of the Crypt get me."

"He's also called the Gatekeeper," Aerdeca said. "If that helps any."

Aaaand damn. Just our luck that the person we were looking for was *also* the freaking Master of the Crypt.

"It does help. Thank you." I turned and left, Cade following.

"Be careful!" Aerdeca called after us.

"Don't lose your head!" Mordaca added.

"Literally." Aerdeca's tone was deadpan.

"I'll try not to!" I shouted back.

We hurried down the street, turning at The Banshee's Revenge, which was heaving with people this close to evening. The next left took us down a narrow lane by some rickety old houses. Most of them looked abandoned, but yellow eyes peered out from behind the boarded up slats of one window.

"This place gives me the creeps," I muttered.

"It's about to get worse."

I staggered, nausea rolling in my stomach. The sun was behind the horizon now, making it harder to see ahead of us, but I'd bet the buggy that we were nearly to the cemetery.

Ten more steps revealed a tall iron gate set in a gap in a tall stone wall.

"Bingo." Cade's voice was rough, the nausea no doubt hitting him, too.

"No wonder people don't like to come here," I said.

"The Master of the Crypt might have had something to do with keeping them away."

"Definitely." I looked up at Cade. "Ready to transform?"

"Aye, though I don't fancy spending much time as that bastard, Cocidius."

"I know."

We'd decided that the best course of action would be to use my illusion power to impersonate Cocidius and Rowan. With any luck, we could trick the Gatekeeper into helping us get to the Rebel Gods main realm. Since Cade was a Celtic war god like Cocidius, we hoped that his magic would fool the Gatekeeper. I'd just have to keep mine under control and hope he didn't figure me out as well.

"Right. Here it comes." I envisioned us changing, becoming other people.

In front of me, Cade's handsome features shifted to form those of Cocidius. The ugly god appeared, his golden horns gleaming in the light.

"How about a kiss?" Cade said.

I stifled a chuckle.

"Actually, I retract the request," Cade said. "Now you look like your sister. Too strange."

A louder laugh tried to escape, but I bit it back. "You're sure I look like her?"

"Aye. And from the grimace on your face, I can tell that I definitely look like Cocidius."

"Well, pretend to be a jerk and it'll help."

He saluted, a gesture that I was sure Cocidius had never made.

I turned to the rusty iron gate and pulled, yanking hard when it stuck solid.

Cade's big hand closed around the metal above mine, and I stepped out of the way. One yank, and the gate opened.

I stepped onto the dark grass, a shiver crawling over my skin. The graveyard was huge, full of ancient tombstones in every shape and size. The sun had set fully, and old gas lamps had burst to life along the path. Most were broken, but the few that flickered weakly shed a creepy light over the place.

"Why would anyone want to be buried here?" I muttered. "Even the people in Darklane?"

Cade stepped up next to me, his wary gaze searching the headstones. Fog twined around them, concealing much of the ground.

"I've seen this place in movies," I said. "Twenty bucks a hand reaches up through a fresh grave."

"Zombies?"

"Definitely." I stepped forward, my skin chilled to ice. The joke didn't do much to make me feel better, but points for trying, right?

A huge, leafless oak rose tall to the left of us. Hundreds of black birds sat upon the branches. One cawed, a sharp screech that rent the night air.

It took everything I had not to race down the path away from the birds. I'd also seen *that* movie, and the birds had won.

I set off down the path, trying to keep my pace sedate. "If he's called the Master of the Crypt, we should probably find one of those."

We walked silently along the path. When several small white buildings appeared in the middle of the graveyard, I pointed to one. Dark magic rolled out from it, a prickling sensation that warned us to go back.

"That one. Feel it?"

Cade nodded.

I fought a retching sensation as I approached the white building. It was one of the larger ones—at least the size of a small house. The white marble was dingy in the light of the moon, and dead vines crawled up the sides.

I stopped in front of the door. "It's solid marble. With no handle."

"Not meant to be opened by normal means." He spun around, studying the graveyard. "We've seen no fresh dirt. This cemetery hasn't been used in a while."

"Probably only used by the Rebel Gods now. We shouldn't force it open, because Cocidius wouldn't have to do that." I studied the dirty marble, searching for any kind of clue.

My gaze caught on symbols carved into the stone. They were randomly placed, and varied in shape and size.

"Hang on," I murmured. "What did Rowan say?"

"'Look for the matching symbols, in order of smallest to largest. Press them.'"

I'd thought it was a strange bit of advice at the time, but now it might make sense. Excitement thrummed in my chest as I studied them. *Yes.* This would work. There were actually pairs of symbols, all different sizes.

Quickly, I pressed my fingers to the symbols in order of smallest to largest. By the time I touched the last ones, magic sparkled at my fingertips.

A pale light glowed, and the door shifted left. It dragged against the ground, sounding like it took enormous effort to open. Dusty air billowed out.

I coughed, gagging on the nasty taste of dust. Bone dust.

Blech.

I stifled the last of my cough and stepped inside the dark room. Pale moonlight filtered in, revealing four stone sarcophagi along the walls.

Cade stepped inside. "Gatekeeper."

His voice rang with command, sounding different in his new form. A shudder ran down my spine. I *knew* he was my Cade, but he sure didn't seem like it right now.

A ghostly figure drifted up from one of the sarcophagi. I blinked.

He had two heads. Or, rather, one head that had two different faces—one facing left and one looking right. One face turned toward us, revealing a fairly normal-looking man with bland features. "Cocidius."

The head turned again, and an angrier face glowered at us. It hissed, "Why do you come here?"

"Manners, Past," said the other face.

"Shut up, Future."

Past and Future?

Janus. The two-faced god of the Romans. Also a gatekeeper, if I was remembering correctly. But he was a ghost? And working for the Rebel Gods?

Dang, they were powerful.

"We require passage to the headquarters of the Rebel Gods," Cade said.

I stood quietly, trying to look unobtrusive. Rowan had looked like a statue most of the times I'd seen her, heavily enchanted.

Janus drifted closer, the head swiveling as the two faces fought for control.

"Something is different about you," Future said.

"Strange," hissed Past.

The two faces were supposed to look toward the future and the past. But their roles seemed to have shifted a bit. It seemed like they were playing Good Cop/Bad Cop with us.

Janus stopped right in front of us, sniffing. Both faces gasped at once, and my stomach dropped.

Oh, fates.

The charade wasn't working.

"You are a Celtic god, but not Cocidius," Future said.

"Impostors!" hissed Past.

Double crap.

Past was definitely the bad cop.

"They may have a good reason," Future said. "I sense honor on them. I like it."

"Of course you do," hissed Past. "But we can't allow them to pass. We have a job."

Future sighed. "Of course."

Magic surged on the air, making my stomach turn and sweat break out on my skin. Janus swelled in size, his ghostly figure doubling in the course of a moment.

I gasped and stepped back. Cade drew his sword, but I didn't bother.

Death.

Janus was the god of beginnings and endings—and he would end us. One touch from his ghostly form and we'd drop like flies. I could feel it in his magic. The stink of decay followed by the smell of fresh earth.

Mordaca had been right. He killed with a touch.

This was a god of many powers—powers that were impossible to fight.

3

"Back up," I murmured.

Cade nodded and stepped back. He sensed it, too. Some things in this world could not be fought on an even playing field. I grimaced as my heart thundered impossibly hard.

We had to convince them. But what did they want?

Nothing.

We had nothing to offer a two-faced god who was bent on performing his role of Gatekeeper.

Janus's huge form drifted forward, arm outstretched. We were near the door—we could run.

But it wasn't an option either. We *needed* him to lead us.

Panic fluttered in my chest. My tongue felt thick.

Then it moved. My tongue moved...*without my permission.*

I nearly screamed.

Speak.

The voice spoke in my head, low and deep. My tongue twitched again. Oh, crap. I was so not doing that!

Speak.

"Hey!" I shouted, startling myself. I had no idea what to say.

It was almost as if my body had just shouted for me without control of my mind.

Janus stopped dead in his tracks.

Whoa.

All right. I could work with this. "Turn around."

Janus spun, facing the other way. Tension vibrated along his enormous ghostly shoulders. He didn't want to obey me, but he was. He *had* to.

"What are you doing?" Cade asked.

"No idea." My mind raced. A new power was clearly coming online—but what? "Who is a bossy Norse god?"

"Odin?" Cade said.

It clicked. "Of course. Odin can speak with the dead. Command them, even."

"And Janus is a ghost."

"I can hear you," Janus said.

"Well, hear this," I said. "You're going to take us to the portal to the Rebel God's headquarters."

"They don't call it their headquarters," Janus scoffed. "Such a modern word."

"Well, I'm a modern gal. Now, you're going to take us there." I dropped the illusion on Cade and me. No need to waste the magic if it wasn't working anyway. I had a new trick. "And shrink down to normal size."

Janus shrank immediately, turning to glare at us. Well, Past glared at us. The grumpy, mean one. Future smiled.

"I don't entirely mind this, you know," Future said. "All day long we fight for control. At least we're not fighting now."

"Ninny," Past growled before turning to us. "You know, this isn't going to be easy. You don't have clearance to walk this path. I can't guarantee you will get through alive."

"I'm used to danger." I grinned. "Now, lead on."

Past harrumphed. "Don't say I didn't warn you."

"Wouldn't dream of it," I said.

Janus led us from the crypt. The night had grown darker and colder, but the ghost didn't seem to mind. He led us around tombstones and tree stumps, stopping in front of a tiny crypt that looked about a thousand years old.

No way that was possible, though. It was a European-style building, and they hadn't arrived here until the 1800s, as far as I knew.

Apparently, being a portal to an evil realm was hard on a building.

"This way," Past grumbled.

We followed him into the crypt. Inside, there was a wide set of stairs. Claustrophobia hit me as soon as we started to climb down.

My breath grew short, and I tried desperately to control it.

"Are you all right?" Cade murmured from behind me.

"Fine." I never got claustrophobia. But these stairs....

The dark magic that lurked in here made me feel like I was trapped in a grave. And the stairs were endless. We walked for what felt like miles.

"How much farther?" I asked. "It's been at least twenty minutes."

My thighs burned, and I couldn't imagine trying to hike back up.

"A while." Past cackled.

It was over an hour before we reached the bottom. My skin was damp with sweat by the time we arrived, but at least the fear had faded.

"We must be more than a mile underground," Cade said. "Is that even possible?"

"With magic, anything is possible," Past said.

"This way now. Don't dawdle, or they'll get you!" Future added.

"They?" I mouthed, glancing at Cade.

He shrugged and drew his sword. "We'll find out."

I set off after Janus, who led us through the large tunnel. A pale white light shined from the ceiling, shedding an eerie glow over the place. The tunnel grew wider as we walked, finally opening up onto a street that reminded me of the Vaults in Edinburgh.

But it was *much* larger.

And full of ghosts.

We stepped onto the main street, which was bordered on either side by small buildings. People flitted by the windows within, and the sounds of life filtered past.

"Who are these people?" I studied the inside of a tavern, where ghosts caroused around a band that played in the middle of the room.

"The music is bloody awful," Cade said.

"The dead aren't as particular," Future said. "These are the souls of those who once worshipped the Rebel Gods. Their magic helps fuel the portal now. And protects it from unwanted visitors."

"Like you." Past turned to glare at us.

I ignored him. "Where is the portal?"

"Farther along." Janus picked up the pace. Future glared at a figure that stepped out of the house to our right.

The ghostly man was dressed in ancient robes, his face looking like it'd been hewn from stone. His gaze landed on us, then his eyes blazed with interest. "Intruders."

"No," Past snapped. "You are confused."

"Intruders." The man stepped closer to us.

Cade held out his sword, tip pointed toward the man's belly. He ignored it, stepping forward again. The blade pierced his stomach, but he didn't seem to notice.

"Get us out of here alive, Janus," I commanded. Magic flowed out from my tongue, sparkling across the tip.

This was one badass power.

"Don't touch the ghosts," Past said. "Else you will become one."

Shit. "Deadly touch?"

"Precisely," Past said. "Like mine."

Cade yanked his blade out, and we hurried on. I glanced back over my shoulder, heart pounding.

The man followed us slowly, brow creased.

"Is this what you meant by the path not being easy?" I asked.

"Exactly," Future said. "I am your guide. An escort. Not a ticket in. If you aren't a Rebel God or one of their invited, there will be protective enchantments to stop you."

"Therefore, I highly recommend that you cease your hold on me and depart this fool plan!" Past said.

"Sorry, pal, can't do that." I peeked back again.

The man had gained on us. He hadn't given us much head start to begin with, so he'd be on us again any second.

"Stop!" I commanded him, feeding my magic into the order.

The words sparkled on my tongue, and the ghostly man halted. He scowled.

Then he howled.

Oh, shit. "Be quiet!"

He snapped his mouth shut, but it was too late.

Figures had spilled from the doors. Men and women, all in different types of dress. All of different cultures. There were dozens.

They stared at us, brows creased. Then they surged forward.

My stomach dropped and my skin chilled.

"Stop! All of you!" I called.

They stopped dead in their tracks, tension vibrating around

them. They wanted to move. To stop us. But as long as I had my magic, they couldn't.

But I was too smart to get cocky.

"Hurry, Janus," I said.

We raced through the town, moving as quickly as we could past buildings of varying styles. My heart thundered as we ran.

The ghosts stood in doorways and peered out of windows. They sat on benches and leaned against walls. Whatever they'd been doing when I'd commanded them to halt, they'd frozen in that position.

I told more to stop as we continued our way through the town. Eventually, I thought I'd frozen every single one.

But all of them peered at us with hungry expressions, making my skin crawl.

Then one of them broke away from my command, stumbling away from the wall and lurching toward us. His eyes blazed with pale light as he reached out for me.

"Back!" I said. "Don't attack."

He froze solid, but another one broke free of my hold, lunging up off of a stone bench.

There were too many. My magic was too new. I could control some, but not all. They strained against my bonds, fighting hard to break free.

Sweat broke out on my brow. "Don't move!"

It didn't do much good. They still fought and pulled. My magic was still shaky. Still new.

"Run, Janus." I sprinted ahead.

As if that was their cue, the ghosts roared and broke free. The swell of their dark magic made me shudder and gasp. I nearly stumbled, but picked up the pace, Cade and Janus at my side.

I could no longer control all the ghosts in town, so I turned my magic toward Janus, making sure he obeyed our commands. We needed our guide, no matter how crappy he was.

"Get us out of here, Janus," I said.

"We must get to the edge of town. They cannot pass the borders."

I sprinted, dodging the grasp of a ghostly woman with long, tangled hair. The chill of her touch froze my arm where she brushed me, and the muscles stopped working.

Fear lanced through me.

One taste of their touch was enough to make me sprint faster than I ever had. Even Cade looked pale next to me.

The ghosts trailed us by only a few meters, thankfully no faster than they had been in their human form.

Sweat rolled down my temples as I ran and dodged. "Go faster, Cade!"

He could outrun me, but he never would. Instead, his magic swirled golden around him, and he shifted into his wolven form. The massive beast galloped alongside me, and I leapt onto his back, grabbing handfuls of fur and scrambling up.

Cade leapt forward, racing away.

"Come on, Janus!" I cried.

At least the ghosts couldn't kill him. He was already dead.

Cade sprinted past the last building in town and carried on for another twenty yards before spinning around. Janus sprinted across the border, but the ghosts pulled up short at the edge of the last building. They appeared to slam against a barrier, their transparent faces flattening against an invisible wall.

Janus panted as he stopped next to us, both faces a slightly darker shade of ghostly white.

"I am officially no longer interested in this endeavor," Future said. "I side with Past. We want no part of this."

"Sorry, pals." I jumped off of Cade's back as he shifted to human. "Let's keep moving."

They both groaned.

"You're not going to like what you find," Past said.

"I'll be the judge of that."

They both huffed, then tromped onward, leading us across a flat stretch of land that looked like it had once been a field. All grass was gone, however, and the air around us shimmered with gray light. It was impossible to see far into the distance. We were still deep in the earth, but it seemed like we were in such a large cavern that there were no walls or ceilings.

My muscles twitched as we walked, as if they were ready to leap into action at any moment.

"Feel that?" Cade asked.

"Yep. Not a fan."

"Repellent charm," Past said. "You aren't welcome here."

"Trust me, I'm super aware," I said.

We pushed onward, fighting the compulsion to turn back. By the time we neared a looming cliff wall, my skin was crawling. The mist parted as we got closer, and I forgot any nerves when I caught sight of the two massive stone lions guarding a gate.

They were at least forty feet tall, each sitting next to a massive door. They glowered at us.

"These were what you said we wouldn't like?" I asked.

"Precisely." Glee echoed in Past's voice.

"No big deal," I said. "We just have to fight some lions."

They roared, surging forward to stand upright on all four feet.

"*Some* lions?" they growled in unison.

"Some special lions?" I drew my sword and let my wings unfurl from my back.

This was not ideal. I didn't want to kill lions. Not even stone ones.

"We are Aker, the guardians of the gate!" they roared.

"Aker?" I looked at Cade.

His brow creased. "Egyptian?"

"Of course," they said.

"So we have to get past them," I mused. We were still a good fifty yards away, but they didn't seem inclined to charge.

"Have you got a riddle for us?" Cade called.

"We are not sphinxes!" they cried in unison.

"You sure?" I asked. A riddle would have been great, because I had no idea how to fight them.

They roared and prowled forward.

I turned to Janus. "Any tips?"

"None," Past said. "If you were an approved visitor, they would open the gate for you. But you're not."

I turned back to Cade. "We can try for speed. I'll distract from the air, and you sprint through as a wolf. Try to break down the door."

Cade nodded. "I agree. We can't fight stone, so speed is our best chance."

"Help Cade," I commanded Janus.

He growled but nodded.

I shot into the air, flying straight for the lions. They roared and charged me as I neared. Right before their stone jaws would have clamped around me, I darted upward, my wings carrying me high.

The lions roared.

I dived low, and they lunged again.

If I could just get them excited enough to follow me away from the gate, then Cade could slip through.

As the lions lunged for me, I dived and dodged. Their stone eyes gleamed with excitement and they charged me, but they did not move far from the gate.

My heart pounded and my breath came short as I pulled out every flying trick in the book.

Cade waited in his wolf form, but my plan wasn't working. Not quickly, at least.

"I'm tasty!" I called. "Excellent with ketchup!"

Not that stone lions knew what ketchup was.

And why the heck were they down here anyway? Shouldn't they be guarding an Egyptian temple somewhere?

The Rebel Gods were good at recruiting to their ranks, but I couldn't see what was in it for the lions.

I flew upward and dived again, flying away from the gates. One of the lions got so excited that he charged farther than he ever had.

Then he stopped abruptly, pulled backward.

I stopped and stared, hovering just out of reach. I peered hard at the lion.

"Is he chained?" I called.

"I don't know," Janus said.

I studied the air around the lion's neck. It shimmered slightly. A collar concealed by magic.

The lions were never going to go far enough from the gate.

They couldn't.

I flew back to Cade and landed. He shifted into his human form.

"This won't work," I said.

"They're captives." He growled.

I didn't like it either. "Hey, Aker! Why are you down here? Why guard this gate? Seems pretty miserable."

The lions stopped and stared at me.

"Why?" they demanded. "Because we do!"

"You're chained," I said. "You can't possibly want to be here."

"Of course not," they said. "But we've tried for decades to escape. Only a god who is not bound by them can break these chains. And if we don't defend the gate, they won't feed us."

I glanced at Cade. "Think you can handle this?"

He flexed his hands. "Definitely."

I turned back to the lions. "Then how about we cut you a deal?"

"A deal?" Both lions cocked their heads.

"Cade here is a god. He'll break your chains. You escape. We go through the gate."

The lions considered.

"How do we know that we can trust you?" they demanded.

"You can always just eat us," I said. "Not like we can kill you. You're made of stone."

They nodded, agreeing that I had a great point.

"We have no loyalty to the Rebel Gods. Break our chains, and you may pass."

I grinned, then pulled up short. "But one thing. You have to promise not to eat anyone in Magic's Bend when you go charging up the stairs."

The lions glowered.

"Go to the Apothecary's Jungle," I said. "Ask Aerdeca and Mordaca to help you get back to Egypt."

"They're going to hate you for that," Cade muttered.

I grinned. "They'll put it on my tab."

"And if you don't want to go back to Egypt, I'm sure they'll make a place for you at the Undercover Protectorate," I added.

"Agreed," Aker said.

Cade stepped forward.

I held my breath as I watched him climb up onto one of the lion's backs. The other lion looked at him like he was a tasty snack.

"Don't go back on your agreement!" I called. "He's the only one strong enough to break you out of here."

The lion grumbled, but sat back, his stony gaze never leaving Cade.

Cade felt around on the lion's back, then picked up an invisible chain and yanked. From the way his hands flew apart, I assumed he snapped the chain in two. The lion beneath him leapt away so fast that Cade tumbled off his back, barely managing to land on his feet.

The freed lion rampaged around, joy in every movement.

The other lion grumbled impatiently.

"I'm coming." Cade climbed onto his back and found the chain, then snapped it. This time, he was quick enough to jump off before the lion leapt away.

"Thank you!" the lions called as they raced away.

"Remember!" I yelled after them. "No eating people in Magic's Bend!"

They roared, and disappeared into the dark.

I turned to Cade. "I *really* hope they listen."

"Their honor will demand it," Cade said.

I liked that he had faith in them. I did, too. If I hadn't, this plan would have been super dumb. We'd have broken their chains, and they'd have bitten our heads off.

Talk about a bad deal.

I looked at Janus. "What's past this gate? The portal?"

He nodded. "Yes, but I've never entered the portal."

"Truth?" I used my Odin's gift to compel him.

"The truth."

Damn. "Then you can't guide us on the other side. But can you tell us what to expect? Where we might find information?"

He shrugged. "It's a large place. Avoid the gods, naturally. And I've heard that there is a place called the House of Wisdom. It will be a building built in the medieval Arabic style. It was constructed in Baghdad in the eighth century AD as the most fabulous house of learning the world had ever seen."

"The Rebel Gods stole it?"

"First, the gods saved it. The Siege of Baghdad in the thirteenth century nearly destroyed it. To save the knowledge, the gods took all the texts from within. Later, the Rebel Gods stole it from them. They may keep records of their plans there."

"Thank you." I made sure Odin's gift was working. "You may go, but *never* speak of us."

He nodded, both faces scowling, then left, hurrying away as quickly as he could.

I turned to Cade, who was already walking toward the massive doors. He pressed his hands to them, pushing hard. His muscles strained, veins popping.

Finally, the door creaked open, the heavy stone swinging slowly inward.

Magic rolled out at me, a tidal wave of sensation that made me shudder and gag. It slimed against my skin and smelled like mildew.

Oh, hell. I did *not* want to go in there. Every cell I had screamed to turn back.

Run.

I sucked in a breath and stepped forward.

4

"Gross." I held my nose and continued toward the darkened room.

"That is some very dark magic." Cade grimaced.

"No kidding." I stopped at the threshold to the room that was shrouded in shadow.

A portal glimmered within, a sick neon green that pulsed with light.

Cade joined me. "What do you think? Should we adopt Eris and Cocidius's forms? Or go invisible?"

"Invisible, I think."

He nodded and reached for my hand.

I gripped his, then turned to him, meeting his gaze. "Thank you for doing all of this with me. The past month. I know it's not your job."

The corner of his mouth quirked up. "I don't spend time with you because it's my job."

"How about risking your life by jumping onto stone lions?"

"Certainly not that." He cupped the back of my neck, leaning down slightly. "You're special, Bree. Not just to the world, because of what you are. But special to me. I've never met anyone like you. I'm sure I never will again."

"I'm certain that's not the case."

"People as strong, brave, selfless, kind, and smart as you are don't come along every day." He pressed a kiss to my mouth, short and sweet. "Or every century. Every millennium."

I glowed. "Well, I won't fight you on that. I might not agree, but I like that you think it."

"Always." He nodded toward the portal. "Let's go do some recon. Then we can take out the bad guys and save the day."

"Save my butt, more like."

He chuckled. "That is highest priority. I'm quite fond of your butt, along with the rest of you."

I grinned and stepped toward the portal, my hand gripped in his. As we neared it, I called upon Loki's power, making us invisible. The magic shivered over me, and Cade disappeared at my side. His hand was still warm and solid in mine, however, and we stepped through the portal.

The ether sucked us in, throwing us across space and maybe even dimensions. I barely understood how the godly realms worked. I'd never been great at science—never had much chance to learn—but they relied as much on magic as anything else.

Frankly, I wasn't sure anyone *really* understood it.

When I stumbled out of the portal on the other side, the dark magic that permeated the gods' headquarters made my stomach churn.

It was dusk here, the sun casting a golden glow over the massive Roman Forum that we'd entered. Huge buildings and gleaming white columns surrounded us. Massive stone slabs made up the ground, and the place was largely empty.

Cade and I stood silently, inspecting our surroundings. A few people walked underneath a covered archway about a hundred yards in the distance, but they didn't turn to look at us.

"No Arabic-looking buildings," Cade said.

"Let's explore."

We set off, hand in hand. It would have been a romantic stroll if not for the danger that prickled in the air and the tension that pulled at my skin.

Carefully, I drew my sword from the ether.

In the distance, between two large buildings, I caught sight of more color. I called on Heimdall's power and focused my super hearing, picking up the sound of revelry.

"Toward those buildings." I raised our joined hands to indicate to Cade where we should go, since he couldn't see me point an invisible finger.

We set off, hurrying past a huge fountain and a column-fronted building. A man in a toga stepped out, his hard face searching the area where we walked.

My breath caught, and I stopped dead in my tracks. Cade halted near me, so quiet that I couldn't even hear his breathing.

Please don't see us. Please don't see us. Please don't see us.

I repeated the mantra in my head, praying that the jig wasn't up. If we were caught this far from our goal, we'd never succeed.

The man scowled, then shook his head and walked off.

My muscles turned to jelly. *Thank fates.*

We took off again, leaving the Roman Forum and entering what had to be the territory of a Mayan god. Two large, blocky pyramids sat across from each other, the setting sun lighting them in gold. Between them, hundreds of revelers danced around fires, all wearing fabulous masks and colorful outfits. Music flared, drums and flutes and other things I didn't recognize.

It was cool though. We were *watching* a piece of history, forever preserved in this godly realm.

"Each god has his own space here," I murmured. "That must be it."

"Aye. But that crowd is too thick to sneak through while invisible. We'll knock into people, and they'll get suspicious."

"Agreed." I tugged his hand, leading him toward a large growth of palms that clustered near the base of one of the pyramids. Once inside, I let go of his hand and stashed my sword in the ether. "I'll transform us into partiers. The masks will hide us."

He nodded.

I called on Loki's magic, and replaced our invisibility with fabulous Mayan costumes and masks. I took his hand again—no way I wanted to get separated in that crowd—then hurried out.

We joined the crush, immediately assaulted by heat and body odor. I breathed shallowly as we weaved between people, trying to avoid the flailing arms and knees of the dancers.

It was impossible, though. The mass of people was nearly impenetrable. Occasionally, someone would look at me weird, and I'd try out a crazy dance move.

I probably looked ridiculous, but it seemed to satisfy them. Honestly, no one seemed that into the partying, so maybe they didn't think it was weird that we were being lazy about it, too.

Until one person grabbed me by the shoulders and pulled me close.

Dark eyes blazed from behind a brilliant red mask. The figure hissed, "Intruder!"

I stopped breathing. The hands tightened on my arms. Cade turned toward us.

We couldn't fight this woman. Not without igniting a massive brawl amongst the thousands who were here. Then the gods would be onto us, and the mission would be a failure.

And we'd probably end up dead.

Nope, not a good plan.

"No." I shook my head. "Not an intruder."

"You invade for information." White stars danced in her dark eyes, not terribly different from Jude's.

But this woman was a seer. I could feel it in her magic, a sense of knowing and seeing.

"Do it. Succeed." Her voice was desperate. "We dance forever for the Hum Has, a Mayan god of death. Destroy them and free us."

"Oh, yeah. Of course." Oh my fates, I sounded like an idiot.

"You have our word," Cade said. "On our honor."

I shot him a grateful look. He sounded much more reliable.

"If we destroy them, you're free?" I asked.

She nodded. "Their magic ties us here."

"Okay. I promise." I squeezed her arm. "Can you tell us where to find information?"

"In the palace of the Agni, the Hindu fire god."

"Where is that?"

"Two—"

A dancer slammed into her, driving her away from us. She was caught up in the crowd that danced endlessly around the fire, dragged away into the darkening night.

I turned to Cade, squeezing his hand tight. "Let's go."

We hurried through the crowd, making it to the other side without issue. As we neared the edge and the people cleared out, I caught sight of pale stone buildings outfitted with many peaked archways. Colorful tiles bordered the similarly peaked windows, and the structures were laid out in a very geometric and orderly fashion.

"Looks Arabic to me," I said.

"That one." Cade pointed to a large building at the far side. "Has to be the House of Wisdom."

It was the biggest, so I'd bet money he was right.

We ducked behind another copse of palms, and I used my

magic to make us invisible again. The whole process was probably a bit suspicious if someone were looking, but it was the best I could do. Better than just disappearing into thin air where anyone could see us, at least.

We hurried from the Mayan god's realm and started across the Arabic one. Fine sand crunched underfoot, packed hard by time. A couple of camels loitered in front of a long, low building, but they were neither pink nor did I think they would sprout wings. Veronica and Doug's camels were definitely superior.

As we neared the House of Wisdom, a calm sense of comfort flowed over me.

"Feel that?" I whispered.

"Aye. I think it's coming from the House of Wisdom."

I nodded, then realized he couldn't see me. Dummy.

As we neared, one of the statues near the doors seemed to shift slightly. They were roughly human shaped, blending with the tile behind them. I squinted.

One moved—just slightly.

Damn.

I stopped short, tugging on Cade's hand, then raised our joined fists to point toward the guards. He squeezed my hand once, which I assumed meant he saw them. They blended well, but they were definitely there.

I searched the rest of the building. The moment I spotted an open window about ten feet off the ground, I felt Cade's warm breath at my ear.

I shuddered—an entirely inappropriate reaction given the circumstances—then heard him whisper, "The window."

I squeezed an acknowledgment, and we hurried toward it, our footsteps silent. The guards were a good twenty yards away, but we couldn't afford to make a peep.

At the window, Cade boosted me up. I scrambled through, nearly toppling off the sill and inside. Barely, I managed to grab the ledge and cling to it, but my foot hit something solid on the inside of the building.

My stomach dropped, and I looked down.

Crap!

A burly demon with short black horns glared up, unable to see me but clearly having felt my foot. His magic smelled like rotten fish and tasted like old milk.

I drew my sword from the ether and lunged for him, pointing my blade straight down as I tumbled off the ledge into the building. It sliced his shoulder, and he opened his mouth to roar.

Fortunately, I fell on him with enough force to knock him to the ground and drive the breath from his lungs. He reached for a blade at his hip, but I reared up, raised my blade, and plunged it into his heart.

He twitched, then lay still, staring straight up at the ceiling.

Cade landed softly next to me. "You made quick work of that."

I scrambled off the demon and yanked my blade out of his chest. "Let's hide him. He'll disappear soon, but we don't need to take any chances."

I couldn't see Cade lift the demon since he was invisible, but suddenly the body was in the air, floating toward a large potted palm. It disappeared behind the palm—not totally hidden, but good enough.

"Where are you?" Cade whispered.

I followed his voice, reaching out blindly. My hands collided with his hard chest, and I worked my way down to grip his hand. Not for the first time, I wished that Loki's powers worked like an invisibility charm, allowing us to see each other but making us invisible to the rest of the world.

But beggars couldn't be choosers, and I was grateful for the wealth of magic the Norse gods had given me.

Together, we moved silently down the hall. We passed room after room full of books. All of them were fabulously decorated, the most beautiful library I'd ever seen.

This place was huge. How the hell were we going to find anything in here?

We probably needed to find someone and ask. A ghost librarian like Florian would be perfect. I could command him to do my will.

Odds were slim on that happening, however.

As we walked, I realized that some of the rooms emitted more power than others. Almost like the signatures of those who had been there before.

"Do you feel that?" I whispered. "The power coming from some of the rooms?"

"Aye, but they're empty."

"Maybe it's from gods who were once here."

"Let's find the most powerful one, then," he said.

We searched for five more minutes—poking our heads into different rooms—before finding a room that had the strongest magical signature of them all. It was vaguely familiar.

"Cocidius was here," Cade said.

Bingo. That was it.

We hurried in, finding a space filled with massive tables at the center and books lining walls. Several maps were laid out on the tables, and I leaned over, inspecting them.

My skin chilled.

It was a map of north-central Scotland. All the way up by the sea.

Near the Protectorate.

"They're homing in on us," Cade said.

Oh, shit.

"Rowan said they had a way to track my magic, but that they hadn't figured it all out yet."

"They're close, though."

I swallowed hard and turned, intending to ransack the place until I had all the answers I needed.

The fist flew at my face before I could blink. Pain exploded in my jaw, and I hurtled back against the table.

Cade spun, but a potion bomb exploded against his chest. He keeled over, slamming into the ground with a thud. Two guards stood in front of us.

Ambushed!

While we'd been distracted by the horror of the map, someone had come upon us. *Heard* us.

I rubbed my jaw and tried to rise, everything going in slow motion. If I could see Cade, it meant the pain had shocked me into losing control of our invisibility. *Shit.*

Two guards hovered over Cade's prone form. One turned to look at me. Quick as a snake, he hurled a potion bomb. It smashed into my stomach, coating me in a cold liquid that froze my muscles.

I stiffened, then keeled over, slamming into the ground. Pain flared in my shoulder and hip.

Wait a sec...

He'd hit me. *Before* the pain had shocked me into losing control of Loki's magic.

"How did you see us?" It was nearly impossible to move my jaw, but the words slurred out.

"You think a guard in the House of Wisdom is not equipped to see through invisibility?" The largest guard scoffed, a brutish sound that was at odds with his elegant armor. "We would not be very good guards, in that case."

He had a point. But seeing through invisibility was a rare talent. Definitely not one you saw every day.

I struggled, trying to move as my blood turned to ice. If the Rebel Gods caught us now, we were doomed.

My skin chilled, and sweat broke out on my brow.

One of the guards bent and scooped me up, throwing me over his shoulder. The breath exploded out of me as my stomach was crushed, and I barely caught sight of the other guard struggling to heave Cade upward.

Good luck with that, jerk.

Eventually, they managed, carrying us through the hall and down some steps into a large, darkened basement. The air was cool and damp—strange, for the desert—while the ground was made of pressed dirt. So were the walls, for that matter. This place had been carved right out of the earth.

Yep—twenty bucks they were about to toss us in the dungeons.

Which actually gave me a bit of hope. Better than being taken straight to the Rebel Gods, after all.

"Throw them in," growled the guard who held Cade.

"Don't want to break them yet," the other guard said.

I was inclined to go with his assessment.

Please don't break us.

A moment later, I was tossed into a large, square bin. It was about eight feet across and built of sturdy metal. A chain sagged over the top of it, trailing off to the side wall where it was wrapped around a big drum.

They threw Cade in next to me. Though my muscles were still and unyielding, I wasn't flat as a board anymore. I couldn't move, but at least my body would bend without breaking.

Hopefully that meant the potions were wearing off.

One guard walked to the middle of the room and bent down, heaving as he pulled up a heavy grate on the floor. The other guard shoved at the bin that we'd been thrown into.

Oh, hell no.

They were going to try to shove us in that hole.

I struggled against the potion that bound me. Though my muscles twitched a bit—small victory—I couldn't really move.

"Cade." My mouth took about three seconds to form the sound.

"Bree." His mouth took at least as long.

In the meantime, the guard started to push us across the ground toward the hole. He gave the bin one fast shove, and the thing plunged into the pit.

My stomach jumped into my throat as we plummeted. The bin stopped abruptly about ten feet down, a chain pulling taut.

"This sucks." The words came slightly faster this time, and I managed to twitch my foot a whole inch.

The chain creaked as it began to lower us into the pit. Darkness surrounded us, the dirt wall roughly hewn.

Farther and farther we went. I strained my muscles, trying to get the motion back into them. My foot twitched again, then my leg. Arms. Neck.

"Can you move?" I asked Cade.

"Aye. Mostly."

The bin slammed to the ground, and I peered upward, realizing that it was roughly the same width as the tunnel, leaving us not very much room to climb out.

The rattling of a chain sounded from above.

"Hurry and unhook it," one of the guards muttered.

Oh shit. They were going to drop the chain in on us. No way they'd leave it connected to the top of the pit so we could climb it.

"Get out of the bin!" I strained to move, dragging myself up the wall of the bin.

The chain had to weigh a hundred pounds. More, even. If it landed on us, it'd crush bones without question. Next to me, Cade struggled like a giant, manly newborn calf. I probably looked just as ridiculous, the potion still seeping out of my muscles.

The chain rattled louder from above.

They were dragging it across the floor.

Oh hell.

I strained and heaved, managing to flop over the side of the bin like a fish and wedge myself between it and the wall.

Jackpot.

Cade dropped down next to me just as the chain began to fall.

I watched, heart racing, as it plummeted toward us. It slammed into the bin, making it rattle.

"Oh fates." Sweat dripped down my back.

That had been a near miss. I could heal myself, but the last thing I wanted was some crushed bones to take care of.

"Apparently they aren't concerned with wounding the prisoners," he said.

"Crushing them, more like."

"We won't have long before they alert the Rebel Gods."

Slowly, I stood on shaky legs. The potion bomb had almost faded, thank fates. Cade joined me, looking steadier on his feet.

I perked my ears, using Heimdall's power to listen for the guards' presence. The sound of retreating footsteps drifted up the stairs.

"Let's make a break for it." I climbed over the bin wall and back into our would-be death trap.

The chain was heavy as I picked it up and studied it. "I might be able to fly this to the top. Then you climb it and we deal with the grate that's locking us in here."

"They obviously weren't expecting one of their captives to have wings."

"Dumb." Though it probably meant that the grate was sealed with a big freaking lock.

I unfurled my wings and held the chain tightly, then leapt off the ground. The pit was barely big enough for my wingspan, but I managed to fly upward a few feet. The chain pulled at me, heavier as I got it farther off the ground.

I pushed myself, sweat dripping down my temples as I flew toward the grate above. Every inch that I managed to rise was harder and harder, the chain enormously heavy for my wings.

Frustration beat in my chest.

Finally, I made it, looping the chain through a slat in the grate above and then clinging to it, letting my body weight drag the free end downward and pulling the rest of it taut.

"Are you all right?" Cade called up quietly.

"Fine!" I gasped, just hanging there as I caught my breath and my muscles recovered. My wings burned from the strain of flying.

Once I'd regained a bit of my energy, I was able to loop the chain around itself. It caught nicely, and I figured it would hold Cade's weight.

"Wait down there a moment!" I flew to the top, studying the grate.

A massive lock kept us trapped, and unfortunately, it was on the outside. Too far for my picks to reach if I wanted to handle it myself.

That was a problem.

Scowling, I studied the area around the grate, looking for weaknesses. Now would be a great time for another godly power to come online. There were a lot of them. Surely at least one of the Norse gods had something that could help me with this.

Instead, my magic stayed dormant.

But my gaze landed on a shimmery blue form.

A pug dragon.

My pug dragon.

"Mayhem!"

5

The ghostly pug flew over to me, some kind of large pastry in her mouth. She seemed to have moved on from hams, at least while she was in the godly realm.

"Is that baklava?" I asked.

She woofed low in her throat, careful to keep quiet.

"Think you can help us out of here?" I asked.

In response, she tossed the baklava up into the air, then caught it in her mouth and swallowed it whole. She burped a bit of fire, then turned her attention to the metal grate, bypassing the lock entirely.

She blew a blast of flame at the metal grate, and I flew down, hovering underneath and avoiding the heat of her fire. She went at it for a while, until the grate turned bright red and began to drip.

I dodged it, calling down to Cade, "Watch out!"

Finally, she created a hole in the grate that was big enough for me to shimmy through—without my wings. Her fire was coming in smaller bursts now, though. Clearly, she was running low. We'd have to make do.

"Thanks, Mayhem."

She grinned, then flew off, hovering slightly away. I waited, giving the hot metal some time to cool, then called down to Cade. "You can climb up now!"

I flew up to the grate near the hole and touched it. Yep, cool. I grabbed on, retracting my wings back into my body, then started to do the hardest thing I'd ever done—a pull-up.

I strained to heave myself out of the hole, muscles still aching from hauling the chain. My biceps trembled, and sweat dotted my brow. Though I managed to get myself partway there, my arms gave out a second later. I barely held on to the bars as my weight jerked downward.

Shit.

Was I not going to be able to climb out of here? All the badass magic I could do—flying, for fates sake!—and I was going to be defeated by a pull-up?

Actually, that wasn't that hard to believe. Pull-ups were freaking impossible.

I strained again, giving it everything I had, but my muscles felt like water.

"I'll give you a boost," Cade said.

I glanced down. He'd climbed up the chain, which had thankfully held solid for him.

My pride wanted to tell him no, but fortunately, I had two brain cells to rub together and I was going to use them. "Thank you."

His big hand cupped my butt, and he pushed. I might have appreciated the touch if I didn't feel like I was about to lose my grip and plummet horribly to my death.

Funny how a little thing like that could kill the libido.

With his help, I managed to flop the top half of my body onto the grate and pull myself out. Cade, of course, leapt out of there like a damned gazelle, looking refreshed and strong.

"Thanks." I leaned over, panting.

Mayhem flew low and looked up at me, then gave me a sloppy kiss on the cheek. It tingled and wasn't wet, since she was a ghost, but the effect was the same.

I grinned and straightened. "We're running out of time."

"Aye. Searching the library isn't going to work."

"Man. We just need someone we can ask for directions." Which was ridiculous. Who was going to tell us what we wanted to know?

A thought popped into my head. I looked at Mayhem. "Are there any other ghosts here?"

She yipped and nodded.

Heck yeah. "Can you lead us to one?"

She spun and flew up the stairs. I glanced at Cade, who nodded, and we followed her. Toward the top, I used Loki's power to make us invisible. I left Mayhem in her visible form, since we had to be able to see her to follow, but I tried to make her body dimmer. It was harder to see her, but that would work in our favor.

She led us out of the House of Wisdom and onto the central courtyard. The fountain in the middle burbled as the water glittered in the moonlight. Darkness had fallen completely, and the scent of night-blooming jasmine filled the air.

It was gorgeous here.

Too bad it was built on a foundation of evil.

Mayhem led us across the courtyard to a tall tower. The stairs wound upward, and we followed. At the top, a small round space contained a large weaving loom.

A ghost sat at it, a woman with long hair and a veil across the bottom of her face.

"Don't make a noise," I commanded as I stepped inside, giving my voice a hint of Odin's power.

Her eyes widened and she nodded.

I turned to Mayhem. "Will you go try to find those guards

who tossed us in the pit and distract them? Don't let them get to the Rebel Gods."

A happy gleam entered her eyes, and she spun away, flying out of the room.

"Twenty bucks she's going to barbecue them," I said.

"Aye," Cade said. "It's her favorite sport. Besides hunting hams, of course."

The ghost watched us warily.

"We're here searching for information about what the Rebel Gods are planning," I said. "They are hunting me. Tell me where I can learn more about what they want."

"They meet to discuss their plans in the palace of Agni, the Hindu god."

Just like the Mayan woman had said. "Do you know anything about their plans?"

Her eyes darkened. "I haven't left this room in centuries."

"Do you want to?"

"Of course." She gestured to the loom. "Does this look like something you'd want to do forever?"

"No, it doesn't. Do the Rebel Gods make you do this?"

"Of course. How else would they have rugs to decorate their palaces?"

I wanted to suggest they go to the Rug Depot and buy them from a salesman named Fred or George or Sue, but forcing a ghost into slavery seemed more their style.

"If we destroy them, will it free you?" I asked.

"It would." She laughed. "But you won't be able to destroy them."

"I'd say my odds are pretty good. I've got determination on my side, at least. Loads of it."

"You're not the first one. But if you're so determined, then I'd hurry. From the ghostly gossip that makes the rounds, I believe this is when they hold their weekly meeting."

"Where is the palace of the Agni?"

"His section is right next to this one. You'll find it on the other side of the courtyard. There is a large building—all white, with a blue roof. The room is in there. A balcony on the second floor wraps around."

"Is there a quiet way to get there?"

"If they haven't changed it since I left this room, then there is a stairway through the kitchens at the back."

"Thank you." I turned to go, then looked back. "I really will defeat them. You'll be free. Soon."

She smiled. "I hope to fate that you are correct."

"But in the meantime, don't tell anyone that we were here." I trusted her—at least, I wanted to—but I still gave my voice some of Odin's power so she had to obey.

She nodded, and returned to her weaving.

It didn't take long for Cade and me to find the white building with the blue roof. The Indian god's section was just as beautiful as all the others, though totally different. More fountains glittered in the moonlight, and swans glided across.

Servants—or slaves, more like—swept the paths free of fallen leaves. Fortunately, we were quiet and they were absorbed in their task, so they didn't see us.

This place would be amazing to explore if it weren't saturated in evil of the first order.

We made our way quickly around the back of the building, following the scent of baking bread and savory spices. My stomach grumbled. I'd always liked Indian food, but didn't get many chances to eat it.

Not that I'd be starting here.

Magic rolled out from the windows, a mix of powerful signatures that had to belong to the gods. Most of them were miserable—the sounds of screams, the feelings of grief and loss, the scent of death and decay.

They were all assholes, every one of them. And they were inside this building. If only we had some way to blow it up.

But it was huge—all stone and tile. No way I could create enough lightning to destroy it. And trying would get us caught and killed.

We stopped at the open door and peered into the kitchen. Cade's hand was gripped in my own so I could tell where he was, and he pressed against my back as we peered inside.

A single cook stood over the stove, stirring a pot of something that smelled delightful. Past him, a staircase went up into the darkness.

I raised our joined hands to point to it, and Cade squeezed.

On silent feet, we crept past the cook. I held my breath, my lungs burning. It would be sound that gave us away, and we couldn't afford it.

Not when we were so close.

The cook coughed, making my muscles tense, but he didn't turn to look at us. By the time we were on the stairs, my head was buzzing.

We climbed quickly and silently. Thank fates the stairs were stone and not wood. Creaking would have been the end of us. I worked hard to repress my magical signature.

As we neared the top of the stairs, the Rebel Gods' magical signatures grew stronger. I had to breathe shallowly, not wanting to take the scent into my body.

The collective feeling of their magic made me want to curl up in a ball and hide.

It was the *worst.*

At the top, we reached a narrow balcony that ran alongside the entire perimeter of the wall. It was more decorative than anything, a style that made the interior of the room look even richer. Which was a challenge, considering the amount of gold covering all the surfaces. The narrow balcony was built of dark wood inlaid with gold that twined around the wide posts that reached to the ceiling. They provided a lot of cover, actually.

Quietly, Cade and I stepped up to the rail, making sure to stay as hidden as possible behind the posts. We were invisible, but the guards had proven that didn't always work.

Down below, eleven gods sat around a heavy table that was made of beautiful tiles. One chair was empty—Chernobog?

I hoped this was all of them, because they were terrifying grouped together like this. Their magic nearly sent me to my knees.

If they were in fight mode?

We wouldn't stand a chance.

We would need every ally we could muster to have any hope of winning. And I'd need every ounce of power I could get.

Down below, Cocidius and Eris sat next to each other. Cocidius's large horns glinted golden in the light, and his gaze looked angry. No doubt because he'd lost Rowan. Eris looked as insane as always, her white robes flecked with blood. Red streaks dripped down her face.

I looked at the other gods, trying to identify them. They all wore historic dress, which helped. But there were still ones I didn't recognize.

Did I dare take a picture with my phone?

What if it made a noise?

I couldn't risk it.

Instead, I set about memorizing each one. Features, clothing, power signature.

A slender, blond god was speaking, his blue eyes glinting rabidly in the light. Norse. Somehow, I knew it. I also knew there was no way I'd ever be getting the gift of *his* power.

I listened hard, trying to pick up every word...

"Once she comes into the last of her new power, the spell

will be complete," the Norse god said. "We will find her then. She will be like a beacon in the dark."

"Tracking her through the magic of the other gods." A dark-haired god grinned and sat back. His clothes were simple—brown robes with a heavy-looking golden disk hanging around his neck. "Genius. She is hidden. Her magic is not. Only you could manage it, Hod."

"When she became a Norse Dragon God, the game changed. Became easier." His gaze moved to Cocidius and Eris. "A good thing, given that you lost their sister."

"Her power was weaker, anyway," Cocidius growled. "Not a Dragon God."

"Not yet," Sven said. "But we will hunt the one who is. And her magic will lead us to the magic of the other two. We will wait until Bree has her magic and she is with her sisters. We will be able to sense that their magic is together. Then we will find them in one fell swoop. Once we have all three, their power will be ours. We will walk the earth again. *All* of us. Permanently. But we must have all three of them."

I swallowed a gasp.

Oh, shit.

The only thing protecting the earth right now was the fact that they *couldn't* visit. Not for long, anyway. I knew our Dragon God magic could give them the ability to visit earth—I hadn't realized it could be permanent.

But it could be. If they caught us and took our magic for their own.

"Then we will rule." Eris grinned, her smile manic.

I knew exactly what she had in mind for her time as ruler. Misery. Disaster. Strife.

Everything that she fed on.

All of these gods would wreak havoc.

"The rise of darkness will come," said Agni, the Indian god.

A smile stretched across his face that made my skin chill and my stomach lurch.

At the far side of the room, a door burst open. A man ran in, hair smoking and eyes wild.

The guard.

Mayhem followed, blowing fire at his butt, trying to reach him.

Oh, shit.

That was our cue.

Run, Mayhem! I willed her to hear me. I didn't think they could hurt her, but she needed to get the hell out of here.

As if she'd heard, she looked up and met my gaze. Somehow, she could see me, despite the fact that I was invisible. I shooed her out. She spun around and flew from the room, so fast she was nearly a blur.

Cade tugged at my hand.

I turned tail and followed, running down the stairs as quietly and quickly as I could. Our stolen information was only good as long as we lived to share it.

We sprinted through the kitchen, footsteps silent and forms invisible. The cook was still standing at the stove, back to us. I strained to hear anything in the building, knowing that the guard was probably telling them about us. As far as he knew, we were still in the dungeon, which gave us a bit of a head start.

I hoped it was enough.

My heart thundered as we rushed out of the kitchen and into the dark night.

"I'll shift," Cade whispered.

His hand left mine and his magic surged briefly. I couldn't see him, but I knew that he must have shifted.

His big warm body pressed against my legs, and I jumped on, holding tight to his fur. I crouched low over him as he took off, sprinting around the building and across the courtyard.

I looked behind just in time to see the Rebel Gods spilling out of the main entrance. Cade darted behind a building.

I used Heimdall's power, but couldn't hear a shout of warning from the guard who could see through invisibility.

Thank fates.

Cade charged through the Arabic god's world and approached the Mayan worshippers. There was no way to cut through easily, but we also didn't have the time to sneak through.

What if the gods had already discovered that we were gone? The dungeon hadn't been far from the Indian god's palace.

"Run between them," I said.

We'd knock some over, no doubt, but hopefully they wouldn't realize what was happening until we were through. We no longer needed subtlety the way we had before.

Cade charged into the crowd, expertly darting through the masses of people. We definitely knocked some over, and fights started in our wake, but no one realized this was an escape.

Not yet, at least.

By the time we reached the edge, the shouts had started.

Yep, this had been risky.

But we were so close to the end. Cade sprinted faster, his breath heaving and his body hot as a furnace. I clung tightly, grateful for the ride. I could fly, but then we'd have to separate. Without being able to touch him to know where he was, I wouldn't know if he'd been hurt.

This was safest.

The Roman Forum held far more people than it had previously—some kind of party under the moonlight. Torches gleamed, throwing golden light over the pale togas worn by the attendees.

Cade dodged them all, sprinting through the crowd on silent feet. His breathing grew quieter, and I could only imagine the control it took when he was so out of breath. Fortunately, it worked, and no one heard us as we raced past them.

The portal gleamed green in the distance, situated in an alcove. There were no guards, likely because most of the individuals here were trapped by the gods' power. The rest of them wanted to be here.

The magic pulsed as we neared, and Cade leapt in. The ether sucked us through, making my head spin, and spat us out in the darkened room deep in the earth.

I rolled off Cade's back, panting and sweating, and let Loki's illusion drop. Cade stood in front of me, huge in his wolf form. His eyes were bright and his chest heaved. He turned, ready to keep running.

We couldn't lose our lead.

Mayhem hurtled out of the portal behind us, giving an excited yip. She flew out of the room.

I scrambled to my feet, following Mayhem and Cade. As soon as we entered the enormous cavern where the lions had been, I unfurled my wings and took to the sky.

Below me, Cade galloped, his powerful strides eating up the ground. I flew as fast as I could, keeping up with ease in my Valkyrie form. Mayhem stayed close by my side, her little wings moving in a blur.

The village loomed in the distance, and I knew we'd need to be fast. Cade seemed to be holding back some of his speed, if I wasn't mistaken.

I hoped I wasn't—because he was going to need it.

We crossed the threshold into the village, and Cade sped up, running so fast it was hard to believe. Yep—he'd held on to some energy.

We were a third of the way down the main street before the ghosts seemed to realize we were there. I was well out of reach up here in the sky, but worry for Cade kept my gaze pinned to him on the ground.

By the time he'd reached the halfway point, the ghosts had started to surge forward.

I flew low, commanding, "Stop!"

They didn't seem to be able to hear me.

I flew lower, level with the tops of the buildings. "Stop!"

They halted, gazes turning to me.

I could feel them fighting my power. I focused, pretending I was Odin, trying to muster all the command he would use so naturally. "Don't move!"

They scowled, dozens of faces turned up toward me. Their arms and legs twitched as they tried to break my hold. Cade was three quarters of the way.

Sweat dripped down my temple as I pushed my magic. It weakened, feeling frail inside me. Like a wire about to snap.

And then it did.

The ghosts surged forward.

"Run, Cade!"

He sprinted forward, still a hundred yards from the edge of the village. The ghosts were fast, racing to catch him.

Mayhem swooped low, darting for the ghosts and blowing fire. It repelled a few of them, but her blasts were small.

I flew lower, trying again to command them. "Stop!"

They hardly hesitated, trailing Cade far too closely.

A flash of ghostly white caught my eye, just before pain flared through my left wing. It faltered. Panic tightened my chest.

I looked over, catching sight of a ghost falling to the ground.

Had he jumped off a roof and tried to grab me?

Shit yes, because I was plummeting to the ground, my left wing frozen. Just like my arm had been when a ghost had touched me on the first trip through here.

I slammed to the dirt, pain temporarily stunning me, then scrambled to my feet, folding my wings back into my body.

Only my right one went. The injured one hung off my back, frozen.

Cade was a dozen feet ahead of me, Mayhem darting around him and blazing fire. Some of the ghosts who were surging toward him turned toward me.

Their cold eyes landed on me.

"Don't move!" I screamed, giving it my Odin all.

They stopped briefly, fighting the hold of my magic.

I started to run.

Cade halted, ears pricked as if he could tell I was on the ground now, then spun to race back to me.

"Go!" I yelled at him. One of us had to make it out of here alive to tell the Protectorate what we'd learned.

If we both died....

The Rebel Gods would get my sisters.

I'd never let that happen.

"Go!" I screamed at him as I ran, my wing dragging and slowing me down.

The ghosts strained at the bonds of my magic.

He gave me a withering look—normally, it'd be hard to tell with a wolf. But this was clearly *withering*.

He was at my side a moment later, growling low in his throat.

Commanding me to get on.

I gave him a withering look of my own, but climbed on, my heart pounding. He spun and raced down the street as I clung on, my heavy wing making it difficult.

The ghosts fought my magic, creating a tearing feeling inside my chest. I struggled to hold them, a strange battle of wills. But they broke through, rushing for us.

Mayhem kept up her attack, darting back to blast her flame

at them. I looked behind. She was slower, her fire smaller. She was faltering too. My magic was nearly spent.

"I can't hold them!" I cried.

Cade gave one last burst of speed and lunged toward the border of the town, where the last house stood. I turned around to watch as he kept going, leaving the wailing ghosts behind. They slammed into the barrier and hammered their fists against the invisible wall, unable to follow.

I stuck my tongue out at them, knowing it was totally immature and not caring even a little bit. Mayhem darted after us. Cade stopped and I tumbled off of him, every muscle aching.

I landed awkwardly on my wing, pain flaring slightly. But it felt good to be lying down, so I stayed there. Just for a moment, staring at the darkness. Breath heaved through my lungs as exhaustion stole over me. I didn't want to get up.

Five more minutes, Mom.

I chuckled, but the thought made me sad, too. Made me miss my mom. I swallowed hard and turned to look at Cade.

In a swirl of golden light, he shifted back to his human form, then stepped over and held his hand out to me. I reached up and gripped it. He pulled hard, lifting me off my feet.

My wing hung limply.

I stared at him, both grateful and annoyed. "That was a risk. If we'd both died, no one would be able to tell the Protectorate what we'd learned."

His gaze hardened. "I would *never* leave you to die."

The strength of his words sent a frisson of elation through me. Elation and confusion. He *really* meant that.

But could he really feel so strongly about me?

"Is your wing all right?" he asked.

I shoved away my messy feelings about what he meant and what he felt, and focused on my wing. In the distance, the ghosts wailed.

Grimacing, I tried to lift it, looking over my shoulder to see if it worked. The wing rose up six inches. "It's coming back to life. It'll just take a bit."

"You can run?"

I nodded. Every muscle ached, but we had no choice. "Let's go."

We hurried to the smaller room—or tunnel, rather—and then started up the stairs.

I looked up at the endless flight, remembering how long it had taken to get down. "Oh, man. This is going to be terrible."

"At least we're on earth. It'd be a waste of their energy to follow us here."

He had a point. They could come to earth so infrequently that they'd only do it if they thought they could capture my sisters and me. Right now, they had no idea it'd been a Dragon God in their damned dungeon.

I struggled upward, eventually managing to fold my wing into my back. Mayhem flew without issue, but at the halfway point, even Cade was flagging.

By the time we stumbled out into the graveyard in Magic's Bend, I was about to puke from exhaustion. The only thing that kept me going was the knowledge that we finally had an idea what the Rebel Gods were up to.

And if we wanted any chance at surviving, we needed to figure out how to defeat them.

Immediately.

6

We stumbled out of the graveyard in Magic's Bend without seeing Janus again.

Which was good, because I *really* wasn't in the mood. Every muscle ached and exhaustion tugged at me. As we walked down the street, Cade wrapped an arm around my waist, and I leaned into him.

"I sure wish we had a transportation charm right about now," I muttered. "I'd transport straight to my bed."

Cade chuckled as we turned right at The Banshee's Revenge pub. It was dark in Magic's Bend now, probably near midnight. My strength was flagging as we approached the Apothecary's Jungle. A tiny pinprick of orange light gleamed near the door. I squinted up, catching sight of Mordaca, leaning against the doorjamb and smoking a cigarette. Her long black dress blended with the dark.

"Those'll kill you, you know," I said.

Mordaca arched a perfect black brow. "Really? I had *no* idea." She jerked her head toward the door. "Your guests are in our back garden."

Guests?

Ah, right. The lions.

"Thank you," I said.

She sighed, giving me a pitying look. "You look like hell."

"I feel like it, too."

Cade's arm tightened around me, keeping me upright.

Mordaca stubbed out her cigarette and turned toward the door. "Come in. I'll get you fixed up. You can even sleep in the guest bedroom."

I looked at Cade. "You good with that?"

He nodded, so we followed Mordaca up the stairs. It was late enough, and we were weak enough, that sleeping before reporting back to the Protectorate wasn't a bad idea. And we'd be safe with the Blood Sorceresses.

"This way," Mordaca called from down the hall.

We followed her voice, entering a workshop that smelled like all sorts of magic. Light, dark, and everything in between. A large wooden table sat in the middle. Herbs hung from the ceiling, and the many shelves were filled with bottles and rocks and all sorts of magical instruments.

She selected two pink vials from the shelf and handed them to us. "These will give you a bit of a pick-me-up. Did you get what you were looking for?"

"We did." I drank the potion, wincing at the slightly sour taste. But strength flowed through my muscles, making me feel better immediately. Exhaustion still tugged at me, but I felt a hell of a lot better. "Thanks."

"You're welcome."

She didn't mention payment, which made me wonder if she'd been body snatched. "Why are you helping us?"

"Don't ask so many questions." She scowled. "Do you want to sleep in the guest bedroom? You still look like hell."

"Only if you tell me why you're helping us." I trusted her, but I was still a bit suspicious.

She sighed, so annoyed I thought her head would pop off. "The lions told me what you did for them. I like that, okay? Now do you want the room or not?"

"Yes." I liked curmudgeonly-but-kind Mordaca.

"This way." She led us up the stairs without another word, taking us through a maze of rooms and passages. This place was way bigger than it appeared from the outside. Like, *massive.*

Which made sense, since she'd said they'd put the lions in the back garden. That had to be a big back garden.

"Is this place expanded with magic?" I asked.

"No. It's built into the other buildings on either side. But we left the facades. Don't mention to anyone else how big it is, though. Some secrets are meant to be kept."

"No problem."

She led us into a large bedroom with a big bed. It was done in blacks and reds, reminding me of her.

"If you need anything, forget it," she said. "Aerdeca and I are all the way on the other side of the house."

"No problem." I smiled at her.

"Thank you," Cade said.

She nodded, then turned and left.

"Well, that was unexpected," I said.

"But welcome." He gestured to the bathroom. "You first."

"My hero." I went into the bathroom and made quick work of the shower, feeling much more human when I stepped out.

I put my T-shirt and panties back on, then slipped into the complimentary robe on the back of the door. The black silk was wonderfully smooth, and the red dragon on the back was a cool touch. Mordaca's guest suite was decked out—Elvira style.

I stepped into the bedroom. "All yours."

Cade nodded, and we traded rooms. I climbed into the bed, my mind circling around the memory of Cade rushing back to save me, growling until I climbed onto his back.

The words, "I would *never* leave you," echoed in my head.

By the time he'd gotten out of the shower, the phrase had cycled through my head about a thousand times.

He stepped up to the bed wearing nothing but his boxer briefs, his skin looking warm and just slightly damp from the shower. I stole a quick peek—*wow*—then looked straight ahead as he climbed into bed and turned off the light.

Tension raced across my shoulders. I was tired, but not *that* tired, and his words kept blaring in my mind.

"You came back and saved me," I blurted.

"That's not quite out of character, you know."

"No." It really wasn't. It wasn't the first time he'd risked his life to save me, and unless I was never in danger again, it wouldn't be the last. But it was really starting to sink in that him risking his life for me was my new normal. It'd taken a few examples, but I was catching on.

Only family had ever done that for me.

And Cade....

"You said you'd never leave me."

Wow. I was two for two on blurting out awkward things.

I glanced at him. His face was cast in shadow, but the street lamps from outside sent a pale glow into the room, highlighting his cheekbones and his lips.

He turned toward me, and I mimicked the gesture so that I faced him. The strangest expression was on his face. Tenderness? Something else?

As naturally as the sun rising, his hand came up to cup my face. "You seem confused, Bree. But it's actually really simple. I love you."

"Whoa." I blinked.

"Aye. It came on quickly. I'm still reeling myself." He shrugged. "But then it became obvious. I love you. Seeing you injured...in danger... It tears a hole in my chest. I'd throw myself off a cliff, if it meant saving you."

Tears pricked my eyes. "I—I—"

"You don't have to say it back. That's not why I said it." A wry grin tugged at his lips. "You pulled it out of me, actually."

I threw myself at him, pressing my lips to his. He *oofed* as he fell back against the headboard, wrapping strong arms around me. Warmth and joy and light shined through me as I kissed him, giving it everything I had.

He was hot and strong beneath me, searing my skin as I tried to touch every inch of him that I could. I loved him—I was nearly certain of it.

I definitely cared for him more than anyone other than my sisters.

But I wanted to wait until it was *my* time to tell him. Right now, I was so lightheaded from his words that I could focus only on them. On him.

So I did, kissing him with all the emotion in my heart.

Cade groaned, a low rumble that sent heat streaking through me, and gripped my waist.

The kiss stole every thought I had, and when I rolled off him and dragged him down onto the bed, it felt like the most natural thing in the world.

As it turned out, sex with Cade had also been the *best* thing in the world. When I woke the next morning, my face pressed into his chest and the black satin sheet draped over my hip, I could hardly believe my luck.

Then I realized that I was drooling on him.

Oh, hell.

Surreptitiously, I pulled away, trying to wipe him clean as a blush heated my cheeks. Last night had been incredible. And I followed it up with *this*.

I sat up, unable to take my gaze off him. His eyes opened, and a grin tugged at his lips, making him handsomer than ever.

He did not seem to notice the spit, thank fates.

"Hey." His voice was rough with sleep.

"Hey." I savored this moment—just for a second—then pulled myself back to the present. There would be time in the future for mooning over each other the morning after. I hoped.

But if we didn't defeat the Rebel Gods, there would be no more mornings. "Ready to go fight some bad guys?"

He grinned and pushed himself up, the sheet dipping down to reveal his strong chest. "Aye, ready to make a plan, at least. Then, after I've had a cup of coffee, we can fight some bad guys."

"Perfect."

We dressed hurriedly, stealing glances at each other, then rushed from the room. It was like a maze, trying to find our way out, but we finally managed. We saw no sign of Aerdeca and Mordaca by the time we reached the foyer.

"I guess we'll just send them a thank-you card," I said.

"That will do." Cade pushed open the door, and we went out into the early morning light.

We made our way out of Darklane and onto the main street. Oddly enough, the same purple cab appeared. The green-haired pixie leaned out the window and grinned.

"I was worried we'd have to walk at this hour," I said.

She tapped the side of her nose. "I've got a sense for these kinds of things."

That worked for me. We climbed into the pink leather seat in the back, and she zipped away from the curve, carrying us to the Historic District. She dropped us at the entrance to the appropriate alley, and we hurried inside, heading straight for the portal back to the Protectorate.

The ether sucked me in and thrust me out in the forest. Immediately, I felt the loveliest sense of homecoming. Even in this still-recovering grove, the Protectorate felt like home.

Cade appeared behind me, and we strode out of the forest, our steps quick. The time change meant that it was afternoon here. When we reached the castle, Ana and Rowan were hurrying out the front door.

"Did you sense us returning?" I asked.

"Call it intuition," Ana said. "Did you find anything?"

"We did. Let's call a meeting."

"Arach is waiting for you, actually," Rowan said. "*That* was Ana's intuition."

Ana grinned and punched Rowan lightly on the shoulder. "Caught. We were with her, trying to figure out Rowan's missing magic, when she felt you arrive."

"Come on." Rowan gestured us forward. "Let's go."

We followed them down the hall to Arach's library, joining a crowd of people within. Hedy, Judy, Carol, Ali, and Haris all waited for us.

"That was quick work," Ana said. "You really know how to muster the troops, Arach."

"I've had some practice." She drifted over from her place by the fire, her gaze glued to my face. "Were you successful?"

"I think so. We did find some good information. Hopefully you can help us decipher it."

Arach nodded, and we all gathered around the table on the other side of the room.

"Well?" Arach said.

I leaned forward, spilling everything we knew. Cade filled in the gaps here and there, creating a complete picture for them.

Arach's gaze sharpened. "It sounds like they will find you as soon as you inherit the last of your godly powers."

"And I can't stop that from happening, can I?" Not that I wanted to—but if it meant they'd never find us.... it had appeal.

"It is inevitable," Arach said.

Jude's lips pursed, concern creasing her brow. Her starry eyes met mine, worry in their depths. "Since you can't anticipate when the powers will arrive, the last one could appear at any moment. Then they could ambush you."

I leaned back, slightly queasy. "We'll never win against them if they catch us by surprise."

"And we can't fight them on their turf," Cade said. "It's far too vast, and their advantage would be insurmountable."

"Agreed," Arach said.

"That leaves us in a serious pickle." Caro's platinum hair glinted in the light, and worry gleamed in her eyes.

"Actually, it's worse," I said. "Somehow, my magic will lead them to my sisters as well. Maybe even if we aren't together. So I could leave the Protectorate to protect this place, but there may be no hiding my sisters once they've found me."

"You're not leaving." Jude's words cracked through the room. "You're part of us, and you need to accept it."

Heat seared my cheeks while gratitude filled my chest. I'd been waffling about that, my own insecurity getting the better of me, but she made it deadly clear she wouldn't accept that anymore.

"Thank you." I turned to Hedy. "Is there a concealment charm you can make?"

She shook her head, lavender hair shining. "Not that can protect you from this."

"The only way you'll be strong enough to defeat them is if you have all your powers," Arach said. "Which will, in turn, draw them to you. Forcing the fight."

"A catch-22, aye?" Haris said.

"In the truest sense," Cade said.

Arach leaned forward. "They *will* find you. There is no hiding."

"So we have to bring the fight to them." I stiffened my spine. "Not on their turf. But we at least need to control the timing. A trap and an ambush."

"Aye." Cade nodded. "That'll be the only way to win."

"Then I need to get the rest of my powers," I said. "Is there a way to fast-track that?"

Arach nodded. "Perhaps. You can go to the gods and ask. They may be willing. Though I doubt the magic will come freely."

"Nothing good ever does," I said.

"We need a plan for the ambush, then," Rowan said.

"They'll be coming for the three of us," Ana said. "You especially, Bree."

"Yes," I said. "They said my magic will lead them to us, and they'll strike when our magical signatures are together. They need all three of us for them to walk the earth forever."

"We could be bait, but just sitting around and waiting is dangerous," Ana said. "Not to mention—how do we know *when* they'll come?"

"I have an idea for that," Arach said. "Korynthius crystals act as magnifiers. You could each put your magic into one. The signal would be so strong that the Rebel Gods would immediately sense it."

"Can we get our magic back out of the crystals?" I asked.

"Yes," Arach said. "If you stab them with steel, the magic will flow back into you."

"This is really good," Rowan said. "It makes for the perfect ambush. It allows us to determine the time of the battle, and gives us the element of surprise and a bit more safety. They're drawn to our magic while we are waiting in the wings, ready to attack."

"I like that!" Ana said. "When they arrive, we ambush them from outside. Bree can fly in and get our magic back while they're still trying to figure out what's going on."

I swallowed hard. The plan was good, but it made me nervous as hell. It was the best we had, though. "Where do we find the crystals?"

"There are several places they might be," Arach said. "Nepal, Germany, Japan. All rumor."

"I can perform the spell to transfer your magic," Hedy said.

"And we can go look for them," Rowan said. "While Bree gets her magic. Once we have both, we put the ambush into action."

"I want in," Caro said.

"Of course you do." Ali grinned. "Obviously, we would like to offer our services as well."

I smiled gratefully at them. "It's scary as hell, but it's a good plan. Gives us a bit more safety and the element of surprise."

Cade gave me a look that said very clearly that he didn't like the idea of me giving up my magic—even temporarily. I agreed with him, but it *was* a good plan. The safest one.

"The timing is important, though," Jude said. "If the gods are willing to grant you the rest of your powers, see if they will hold off until we know that Ana and Rowan have retrieved the crystals. We'll need to work fast to put the ambush into action. We don't want the Rebel Gods surprising us before it's set up."

"Agreed." I looked at Arach. "How do I reach the gods?"

"Go to Yggdrasil and try to find them. In this, you will know more than I. It is your pantheon."

My heart jumped at the idea of returning to the World Tree. We'd nearly died so many times on our first visit, but the place was so amazing that I was eager to return.

Cade met my gaze. "I'll go with you."

"Thank you."

"Don't worry," Ana said. "We'll keep in touch using a comms charm. Once we have the crystals, you get your magic."

"Then we'll meet up and destroy the Rebel Gods." There was a bloodthirsty gleam in Rowan's eyes.

Hope flared in my chest. We were still a long way off, but at least we had a plan. A dangerous plan.

But with all my friends and family at my back, this was starting to seem possible.

~

Cade and I had agreed to meet in an hour, giving us both enough time to change and eat. My stomach grumbled as I walked to my tower apartment, Ana and Rowan at my side.

I couldn't believe how amazing it felt to finally have them both with me. Scratch that—I could believe it. And it was *really* freaking amazing.

We entered my apartment. The first thing I caught sight of was a box of crackers on the counter. They were open, which I didn't remember doing.

Then a little black and white head popped out, whiskers twitching.

Boris stared at me, eyes gleaming.

"Cracker thief," I said.

He popped back down into the box, and I could hear the sound of crunching. First the Pugs of Destruction, now Boris. What was it about my apartment that made the animals come here to steal food? Boris hadn't even gnawed into the side of the box like a normal rat. He'd carefully opened it from the top, then jumped in, no doubt feeling like Scrooge McDuck diving into his pool full of gold.

"I thought he lived with Hedy?" Ana asked.

"He does." I went into the kitchen. "I think he just visits for snacks."

"It's not like Hans wouldn't feed him anything he wanted in the kitchen," Rowan said.

"True." I peered into the box to see him lying on his back on top of the crackers, a blissful expression on his little face. "I think he likes the thievery aspect."

His eyes popped open, and he glared at me.

"Perhaps you were just visiting me? Your close friend?" I asked.

He nodded, then closed his eyes and began to snore.

I chuckled and turned away, looking at my sisters. "I'm going to grab a PB&J. Want anything?"

"A candy sandwich?" Rowan asked.

My chest filled with warmth at Rowan's memory of what I called my favorite food. "I'm so glad you're back."

"Me too." She tucked her dark hair behind her ear. "I can't tell you how much."

I started putting together sandwiches for everyone, assuming that they wanted them since they hadn't said otherwise. Ana rummaged around in my fridge, pulled out some energy drinks, and tossed them around.

Once the sandwiches were made, we piled onto the couch to eat, Rowan in between Ana and me. In sixty seconds flat, I scarfed my sandwich down, barely stopping to breathe.

I swallowed the last bite and turned to Rowan. "How's the magic coming along?"

"It's not. It's gone."

"*Gone* gone?"

"If you mean, do I feel like my soul has left the building?" She shook her head. "Still no, thank fates. I just can't seem to make it work."

Relief loosened my muscles. I hated that she was having

trouble with it, but at least all of her magic wasn't gone. That felt like the worst kind of death.

Back at the temple at Kart-hadasht, we'd saved some of her magic that had been in the eternal flame and Nix had put it into a rock strong enough to hold it. But Rowan had been unwilling to even look at it. Some of the Rebel Gods' dark magic was mixed with her own inside the vessel. Whatever she'd gone through with them had been so bad she was willing to sacrifice some of her magic to avoid even revisiting it.

"Are you adjusting okay here?" I asked.

Rowan hesitated, and I leaned back to meet Ana's gaze. Worry glinted in my blonde sister's eyes.

"I am," Rowan said.

"You're lying." I scowled at her.

"Not *entirely* lying. I think I'm adjusting as well as I can. It's not great, but I'm messed up, guys." She rubbed at her forehead, blue eyes shining. "The last five years did a number on me, and I don't trust anyone but you. I know I should. But I don't."

Guilt streaked through me. I needed to remember that she was coming at this from a totally different perspective. If she recovered without debilitating PTSD, this would be a win.

"I'm sorry," I said.

"Don't be. I'm going to be fine." She gestured to the apartment, but I could tell she meant the whole Protectorate. "This place is amazing. We have a real home. I still need to find my place here, but at least we're all together."

I squeezed her hand. She smiled and tugged at her dark T-shirt. She didn't look exactly like how I remembered her. But last I'd seen her, we'd been in Death Valley, and she'd worn the same strappy leather get-ups we all had. She still had to develop her cold-weather style—just like I had.

And she probably needed some time to find herself again.

Find her footing in the real world. She'd belonged to the Rebel Gods for five years. Even her mind hadn't been her own.

"I don't know what it will take to make you recover," I said. "But I'm here for you. For whatever."

She smiled. "Thank you."

"Same, obviously," Ana said. She pressed her side into Rowan.

I leaned over to look at Ana. "Any idea what that white light was about? Back when we were rescuing Rowan?"

We'd explained to Rowan about being Dragon Gods and the powers that were gradually granted to us by a select pantheon, but we hadn't had a chance to talk about Ana's potential new power.

Ana shook her head. "I have no idea what that was. I've tried to replicate it, but failed."

I frowned. "Did you hear a voice when the power arrived?"

"What kind of voice?"

"The kind that tells you to use it. Maybe gives some basic instructions."

Ana shook her head. "Nope. One minute we were going to die. The next I felt like a giant ball of energy, and the light started to glow."

I leaned back against the couch, mulling it over. "I have no idea."

"I *definitely* have no idea," Rowan added.

It sounded like Ana's transition wasn't going to be as straight-forward as mine had been.

"Eh, don't worry about me." Ana pulled her legs up underneath her. "I'll be fine."

She sounded like she believed it. And I was sure she *would* be fine. Ana had the most strength of will of anyone I'd ever met. But I knew she had an iffy relationship with her magic. Defensive magic in an offensive world, she'd called it once. She'd been drunk, which was pretty much the only way you could get her to complain.

Ever since we'd lost our mother, Ana was the poster child for Keep Calm and Carry On. She believed in the stiff upper lip so much that you'd have thought she was British.

Basically, she was too stalwart to whine.

Not me. I loved a good bitch session.

I vowed that I'd help her figure out her powers. As soon as we defeated the Rebel Gods and our lives were back on track, it would be my number one goal. That, and helping Rowan get her magic back.

But first, we had to defeat the Rebel Gods. There was nothing for us if we didn't. Just death, if we were lucky.

But together, we had a chance.

"I love you guys," I said.

As if pulled by gravity, we leaned in and hugged each other.

7

Once I'd changed my clothes, I went to find Cade, who had agreed to meet me in the entry hall at five. Fortunately, we still had several hours of daylight. Thank fates, because I wasn't keen on the idea of climbing down the cliff to the Seer's Cave in the dark.

As I stepped into the entry hall, I caught sight of Cade waiting near the door, Mayhem hovering above his head. She gripped a ham in her mouth, which was really no surprise.

"Ready?" he asked.

"Born ready."

He grinned, then held open the huge door. We made our way out into the warm afternoon sun, then cut across the lawn, passing the stone circle on our way to the cliffs.

As usual, it vibrated with a strange magic. One that pulled as much as it repelled. I wanted to explore, but something told me not to. That place wasn't for me.

I looked away from it and eyed the cliff. The world looked like it ended up here—just dropped right off into the ocean.

We stepped up to the edge, and I looked down. The water crashed against the beach below, blue waves topped with white foam. Light glittered on the surface, and white gulls swooped in graceful arcs.

I shivered at the idea of climbing down, remembering nearly losing my footing and almost plummeting to a terrible death.

"I think I'll fly," I said.

"I'll meet you at the bottom."

I nodded and unfurled my wings, leaping off the cliff. The sea breeze caught at my hair, and the scent of the sea filled me with joy. It reminded me of Cade. And of being free.

I swooped on the air, following Cade down and joining the gulls in their flight.

This was my favorite place to fly—no question. Everything felt so safe and free up here.

I landed on the beach at the same time Cade did, pebbles crunching underfoot. The waves lapped at the shore as we walked.

We rounded the bend and approached the massive mouth of the cave. It was cool and dark inside, the walls gleaming with water and spots of green moss covering some of the rocks within. The little pond in the center rippled softly.

The large rock in the middle called to me, like it had the last time.

"Come on," I said. "We need to climb onto this rock."

At least, that was what I thought. It was how I'd gotten to Yggdrasil the first time, so it was worth a try this time.

I scrambled up onto the giant stone, Cade following. We sat quietly, and magic began to buzz almost immediately. It felt like taking a bath in seltzer water. A golden light flared, and I fell to my knees. Which should have been impossible, since I'd been sitting on my ass, but that was the magic of portals.

When I opened my eyes, I was kneeling in the grass next to Cade.

He blinked and looked up. "That was intense."

"Right?" I followed his gaze, once again awed by Yggdrasil.

The giant ash tree loomed impossibly large. There was no way I could see all the way to the top, and the breadth of it was so wide that I could barely conceive of it.

I stood, using Heimdall's vision to search the base of the tree for the three Norns. I spotted their long house and their well, but they were nowhere to be seen.

Hunting them down was an option, but something was tugging at my chest. A desire to fly upward.

I shifted, but the feeling was unmistakable.

"Do you mind waiting here a bit?" I asked. "I feel like I need to fly upward."

Like I was being called home.

"Not a problem." Cade spun around, wonder in his eyes. "I could spend all day here."

"Thanks." I leaned over and kissed him. "Be safe."

"Always."

I grinned, then unfurled my wings and took off for the sky. Joy surged through me immediately. Forget the cliffs in Scotland. *This* was my favorite place to fly.

The air here was fresher, the breeze lovelier. I flew upward, angling my path toward Yggdrasil's enormous trunk. The branches flashed by as I rose higher. A shimmering portal caught my eye, and I shuddered. If I remembered correctly, it led to Muspell, the land of the Fire Giants.

No thank you.

My instincts were calling me upward, anyway.

It was incredible to fly past the branches and leaves and portals—the whole world. At one point, I saw Ratatoskr, the giant gossipy squirrel, heading toward the ground, his cheeks full of acorns. But something continued to pull me upward. So upward I flew.

When my gut directed me toward the portal leading to the

Valkyrie realm, I wasn't surprised at all. I flew right through without pause, arriving in the same amazing valley as before.

Mountains soared high on either side, and the green valley stretched out in front of me. Sunlight glittered on the river, and in the distance, I could just barely make out the tiny dots that were the buildings in the village.

I headed straight for it, but didn't need to go far. Tiny figures appeared in the air, flying toward me. As they neared, I realized that they were winged horses. Two of them, each ridden by a Valkyrie.

A welcoming party.

I grinned and flew toward the ground, landing mostly gracefully. Certainly not as gracefully as the horses, but it was more important to be on the ground. I didn't fancy a conversation while trying to keep myself aloft.

The horses approached, and the two Valkyrie smiled at me. Each wore shining chainmail, their hair gleaming in the sun. I recognized them from my first visit.

"Bree!" said the blonde one on the black horse. Her name was Sigrún, if I recalled correctly. Which I did. Not like I was going to forget the names of the Valkyrie. "Are you here for a visit?"

"I'd like to be, but no. I need help, and this was the best place to come."

"What is it?" said Gunnr, the red-haired Valkyrie, who I thought was in charge of records or something along those lines.

"The Rebel Gods are hunting me, and I need to be granted the rest of the gods' magic if I want to fight them on even terms. I'm here to request that from the gods."

Both Valkyrie frowned.

"That's not good," Sigrún said. "You've confirmed that they want you specifically?"

"Definitely." I explained how they could track my magic and

would find me as soon as it was all granted. And, on the flip side, I needed that same magic to have any chance at victory against them. If I couldn't control the terms of our final battle, I'd have no chance.

Gunnr nodded, his gaze serious. "Yes. I can see how you would need your magic for that."

"There's one thing you can try," Sigrún said. "I cannot guarantee it would work, but you can go to the *Blót tjörn* at the base of Yggdrasil. Make an offering in the lake. If you are lucky, the gods will take pity on you and grant you a meeting."

"*Blót tjörn?*"

"Sacrifice pond. Ask them for a meeting, then make your sacrifice," Gunnr said.

Sigrún nodded. "Perhaps they will take pity on you."

"What is an appropriate sacrifice?" I asked.

"That is up to you," Gunnr said.

Dang. That would be a hard decision. "And where do I find the *Blót tjörn?*"

"Eighty miles clockwise from the Norns' longhouse at the base of the World Tree."

"Thank you. Truly." My heart tugged. I wanted to stay longer. To visit the village. But there was no time.

"Bree?" Sigrún asked. "You're planning an ambush of the Rebel Gods?"

"Yes."

"As I thought." She nodded. "How many are there?"

"At least eleven. Plus any mercenaries they might have."

The Valkyrie frowned and looked at each other, then met my gaze.

"When the time comes, send word to us," Sigrún said. "We will come join you for the battle."

"*Thank you.*" Gratitude welled in my chest.

This was huge. We needed all the help we could get—and an army of Valkyrie definitely qualified as top-notch help.

"It's a worthy cause," Gunnr said. "We cannot leave our realm often, but for this, we will."

"Thank you, again." I smiled at them, reluctant to leave, but knowing that I had to go. It was a bit like being with my sisters.

But my real sisters waited back on earth, and I needed to do everything I could to keep them safe.

The Valkyrie watched me leave, and I turned back to wave before flying through the portal again.

The flight back down the tree was slightly odd. Miles and miles, tempting me to just close up my wings and do the job quicker by falling. But I'd never tested unfurling my wings while mid fall, and I wasn't going to start now.

As I neared the grass, a large brown spot caught my eye. I flew lower.

Ratatoskr.

The giant squirrel was sitting on the grass next to Cade. His nuts were between them, and I could pick up the lightest bit of discussion.

I landed.

They were deep in conversation, turning only to look at me once I'd cleared my throat.

"Gossiping?" I asked.

"Gambling." Cade pointed to the dice on the ground. "Ratatoskr loves a good game, apparently."

"And always wins!" Ratatoskr crowed.

"Not yet," Cade said.

"But I will."

"What did you bet him, Cade?" I asked.

"Just a growler full of his favorite beer. It's from Edinburgh."

"Thank fates it wasn't your head or firstborn," I said.

Ratatoskr wrinkled his nose. "What would I do with that?"

"Good point." I looked between the two of them. "One more game, because we have a mission to accomplish. But if Cade wins, then Ratatoskr will give us a ride around the base of Yggdrasil."

Ratatoskr scowled. "I am not a ferry service."

"You are today, Your Rodentness."

"Fine! One game, but I shall beat you, puny human."

I thought he would shake his fist, but he just gave Cade a good glare. Cade grinned and picked up the dice. I watched anxiously as Ratatoskr covered his eyes and Cade rolled.

Eighty miles was a long way. If Cade won this, we'd make the journey that much faster.

"Six," Cade said.

I frowned. He had actually rolled an eight, but he sounded truthful. He winked at me.

"Ah, truth," the blinded Ratatoskr said.

Cade swept up the dice before Ratatoskr could uncover his eyes and handed them over. The squirrel took them, his big hand closing around the tiny pieces of carved bone.

Cade covered his eyes and Ratatoskr rolled, then lied about his toss.

"Lie!" Cade said.

Ratatoskr harrumphed, then picked up the dice.

"One life down," Cade said.

"I'll get you next time," Ratatoskr said.

And he did, calling Cade's bluff. They told the truth on the next two turns, but it got interesting after that. My palms dampened as I watched them, worry streaking through me.

Finally, Cade won. On a bluff this time, as well.

Ratatoskr grumbled and picked up the dice, then shoved them into a little leather pouch tied around his waist.

"Why don't we meet again for another game sometime?" Cade asked. "I will bring you some beer then."

Ratatoskr looked at him suspiciously, then grinned toothily, his biggest front teeth gleaming in the light. "All right." He crouched low. "Now hop on. Where are we going?"

I scrambled up onto his furry back. "*Blót tjörn.*"

"Ah, have a favor to ask, do you?" Ratatoskr said.

"Yes."

Cade climbed on behind me, and Ratatoskr took off, sprinting toward the base of the World Tree and turning left. We raced by the Norns' longhouse, and one of them peered out of a window at us.

I waved but she didn't return the gesture.

Ratatoskr leapt over roots and dodged around giant rocks. The wind tore at my hair and made my eyes water. Just once, I dared a glance up at Yggdrasil, but the sheer size of it made my head spin. I looked down and clutched at Ratatoskr's fur. He ran as fast as a car—at least sixty miles an hour, I had to guess.

By the time we stopped in front of a sparkling blue pool pressed up against the trunk of the tree, my arms ached from holding on. I tumbled off the squirrel, barely managing to keep my footing.

Cade slid down effortlessly, of course.

Ratatoskr rose up on his hind legs and gave Cade a hard stare. "Be sure you come back with that beer."

Cade smiled. "You can count on it. And I'll beat you again at *Mia*."

"Beginner's luck," Ratatoskr grumbled, then ran off, straight up the tree.

Cade chuckled and turned to me. "What are we doing here?"

"I have to ask the gods for a meeting and make a sacrifice in that pond." I pointed to the sparkling blue water.

The pond was fairly large, at least a hundred yards wide, but at the base of Yggdrasil, it looked tiny. Pale sand bordered the water, and pebbles gleamed beneath the clear surface. The water rippled and glittered in the sunlight.

I strode up to it, inhaling deeply and enjoying the fresh taste of the air. "I wonder what kind of sacrifice I should make."

"Odin sacrificed his eye to drink from the well of Mímir to gain the wisdom within. But I don't think you should go quite in that direction."

"No, definitely not." I liked my eyes. That would make it a good sacrifice, of course, but it needed to be something different. I frowned, thinking of what was most valuable to me.

The buggy, of course. I didn't have that on hand, however.

But I did have my sword.

My chest ached at the thought. I'd had that sword for years.

My mother had given it to me.

I drew in a ragged breath. That made it perfect.

I pulled the sword from the ether, tears pricking my eyes.

Cade squeezed my hand briefly, and I drew strength from it. I bit my lip. "How do I ask the gods for a meeting? Will they even be able to hear me?"

"Hmmm." Cade studied the pond and its surroundings.

I joined him, inspecting the pond. A few lines in the sand caught my eye, and I walked toward them.

They were the semi-obscured marks of runes. Some Old Norse, as well. And a few drawings. It'd been disturbed, by animals maybe, but it was clear that quite a few people had made requests of the gods. And they'd used all kinds of ways to do it.

I pointed to the marks with the sword. "I think that's what I need to do."

But I had to remember how to write in Old Norse. The ability to read it had developed along with my powers. But I'd never tried writing it.

I concentrated on my memory of reading different texts as I

sought out an unmarred patch of smooth sand. The tiny grains sparkled in the sun, and the water lapped at it.

But nothing came to me. At least, I wasn't sure that the words were right. And I needed to be right about this.

Perhaps a drawing would be better.

Carefully, I used my sword to carve a drawing of myself meeting with the gods. I chose Odin and Frigg, because they were the top dogs. It looked shaky, but it wasn't the absolute worst. They could probably tell what it was.

"Cross your fingers." I drew the sword back, like I was going to throw it underhand, then hurled it into the pool.

My chest ached as I watched it hurtle end over end, finally splashing into the water and sinking deep. Cade appeared at my shoulder, wrapping his arm around me. I leaned into him, sniffing back any wayward tears, then watched the water.

"I have no idea what's supposed to happen," I said.

"I've no idea either."

"Well, I hope they come through." I gazed around, searching for something. Nothing appeared. "Odin! Frigg!"

Silence.

"Loki! Freya!"

Still nothing.

"Heimdall!"

Nothing.

I kicked the sand, but as I looked up, I caught sight of a shimmering patch of air. It glowed like opals, right over the place where I'd thrown my sword.

A portal.

"Maybe you shouldn't have thrown it so far," Cade said.

I laughed, a sound of pure relief, and waded into the water. It was cool and lovely, making me want to swim laps for ages. I struck out for the portal, cutting through the clear water quickly. Cade followed, his strokes strong and sure.

Magic pulsed from the portal as we neared. I sucked in a deep breath and swam straight through it. The ether sucked me in, throwing me across space and dimension. A rainbow of different colors flashed in my eyes, accompanied by a howling wind that dried my clothes and hair.

The ride took longer than any other portal ride I'd ever been on, and felt like traveling the length of the universe.

When I stumbled out into a quiet forest, my head was spinning. Cade appeared next to me a moment later, looking dry but windblown.

I turned in a circle, marveling at the trees around me. They weren't huge, but the white birches glowed with magic. Their leaves rustled in the breeze, and dappled sunlight shined through, sending lovely patterns across the forest floor. Nearby, a river burbled along.

"Where are we?" Cade asked.

"I don't know."

A fluttering sounded from nearby, then the cry of a bird. I looked up just as a black raven hurtled though the leaves and landed on a nearby branch. He looked at me, his dark eyes glittering, and gave a single loud caw.

"Huginn?" I asked.

Huginn cawed again, a clear affirmative.

Odin's raven who had helped me on my last visit was remarkably smaller than he had been last time. Another raven joined him, identical save for a single white feather at his breast.

"Muninn?" I asked.

Muninn cawed, another affirmative.

Huginn and Muninn, representing thought and memory respectively.

I looked at Cade. "I think they are our guides? Maybe Odin sent them to lead us to him."

Huginn and Muninn slowly flew away, but making sure to keep low.

"Aye, I believe you're right," Cade said.

We followed Huginn and Muninn through the lovely forest, eventually reaching the edge. Ahead, a city gleamed. It was built entirely of gold and silver, spires reaching toward the clear blue sky.

Awe streaked through me. "Asgard."

"The Viking gods aren't subtle, aye?"

"Not the Aesir." There was another group of gods called the Vanir, but I wasn't sure what their city looked like. The Aesir sure liked to flaunt their wealth though.

Huginn cawed, a clear statement of "Quit dawdling!"

I hurried to catch up, racing across the field that surrounded the city. Cade kept pace easily, his long strides eating up the ground.

Huginn and Muninn led us to a fabulous gate. There was no door—the Aesir weren't worried about attacks, clearly—but the gate was an impressive status symbol.

My heart thundered as we passed underneath the massive golden arch. Magic vibrated around it, a statement of power that was hard to miss.

We followed Huginn and Muninn through the city. It was impeccably laid out, featuring fantastical architecture that was like nothing on earth. As the ravens led us along, it was quiet, with only a few people passing on side streets. Here and there, fountains shot glittering water toward the sky.

When the birds led us up to a fabulous palace, it was pretty dang obvious who would live inside.

"Odin."

"A safe bet," Cade said.

A huge courtyard sat in front of the castle. Wide steps led up to the massive gate. There was hardly anyone around, however.

"Is it eerily quiet?" I asked.

"Aye."

Huginn and Muninn alighted on top of a fountain in the middle of the courtyard, cawing and beckoning.

We followed, cutting across the quiet courtyard. Nerves began to replace the wonder that had filled me.

It was just *too* quiet.

We climbed the wide steps to Odin's palace. As we neared, magic rolled over me, stealing my breath. I braced myself, determined to provide a strong front.

The doors were huge gold monstrosities. I stopped in front of them, swallowing my fear, and watched them swing open to permit us entrance.

8

The ravens swooped through, leading us into an enormous golden hall. The human Vikings had lived in dark wooden longhouses, but the gods favored an entirely different style.

A woman wearing a green dress appeared through an archway to the side, her long golden hair done up in braids and her eyes shining a similar shade of green to her dress.

She wasn't a goddess—I was sure I would have felt it—but her magic was powerful nonetheless.

"Odin will see you now," she said.

"Um, thank you." That was quick. She'd caught me by surprise, but I was grateful that my sacrifice had clearly worked. At least, it'd gotten me this far.

She inclined her head, then gestured for us to follow. Huginn and Muninn flew behind us, clearly determined to escort us all the way.

The hall that we followed her into was far larger than the first. Silver and gold gleamed from every surface, but it was the massive throne on the other side of the room that caught my eye. It was more like a bench than a single seat, and two people sat upon it.

Their magic rolled across the room toward me. I staggered, catching myself before falling. Cade kept his footing, but he stutter-stepped. The gods couldn't have noticed, but I knew how he normally moved.

Odin and his wife, Frigg, sat upon the throne. She was the goddess of wisdom and foreknowledge, and he was the Allfather —god of war and death. As well as king of the Aesir branch of the gods. They looked older than I expected, both white-haired and lined. Odin's eye patch gleamed gold—covering the eye that he'd sacrificed to Mímir.

Nervousness made my skin crawl as we approached, but I straightened my shoulders. They'd chosen me. That had to make me worthy. I had to assume that, at least, if I wanted to get through this.

And I *needed* what I'd come here for. Not only for myself, but for my sisters. There was no turning back.

The thought gave me courage, and I finished the last steps toward them, determination fueling every one. Cade stopped next to me, and we stared at Odin and Frigg, two of the most powerful figures in the universe.

Dang, but I could feel it. Their magic was nuts.

"Bree Blackwood," Odin said. "You have requested an audience. A rare thing for a mortal."

"I need help."

Odin inclined his head, striking me again as much older than I'd expected. "What is it that you require?"

"The Rebel Gods hunt me and my sisters. To defeat them, I must have all my powers. And I cannot wait for them to arrive one by one."

A skeptical look crossed his face. "That is a most unusual request."

"But she is the chosen one," Frigg said. "She must have good reason."

"I do. The Rebel Gods have a spell that will find me as soon as the last godly power is bestowed upon me. But I don't know when that will be. If I can control the timing of that—and get all the powers at once—I can manipulate the final confrontation to be in my favor. And I'll have the strength to defeat them."

"So you want to control the timing of these gifts as well?" Odin's white brows rose. "That is quite bold."

"I know. But I have to ask. There is so much at stake."

"You are correct in that," Frigg said. "The gods gifted you with their powers for a reason. If you die before you can fulfill it, then what was the point of it all?"

"I think defeating the Rebel Gods is the reason," I said.

Frigg nodded, seeming to agree. Her gaze landed on Cade. "And you travel with another god?"

Cade stepped forward. "I am Belatucadros."

"Ah, Celtic god of war." Odin looked at him appreciatively. "An earth-walking god."

"You must be quite strong to bear that burden," Frigg said.

Cade just gave a small smile and inclined his head.

"And you accompany our Valkyrie." Frigg looked at me. "That speaks in your favor."

"I think my own actions speak in my favor," I blurted.

Ah, crap.

Maybe that hadn't been wise.

But Frigg just smiled, finally showing me something other than skepticism. My shoulders relaxed the tiniest bit.

"I can consult the fire," Frigg said. "Fate will determine if it is possible to give you your magic early. It will also direct how you will become worthy of that gift. I can give you no details about the outcome of your efforts, but I can guide you a bit."

Odin nodded, clearly his official stamp of approval.

"Thank you," I said.

Frigg rose, her movements graceful but slow.

Why the heck were they so old? They looked nothing like all the images I'd seen of them. True, those were artists' interpretations, but this was a bit weird.

She drifted past us toward the middle of the large room, stopping there and waving her hand so her magic flared. It sparkled through my mind, like my head was full of champagne. I shivered.

Weird.

A large golden basin appeared in the middle of the floor in front of her. It was at least ten feet across, and gleamed in the light of the fiery chandeliers above.

She knelt and made a complicated series of hand movements. Again, her magic filled the room, rolling across my skin and through my mind. Soft words drifted across the hall, and I realized she was talking, her lips moving hardly at all.

A massive blue flame burst to life, reaching nearly to the ceiling. The heat seared my face, and I stumbled backward, then glanced back to Odin, who didn't seem the least perturbed.

Apparently he was used to his wife's intense brand of magic.

The flame died down, leaving curling white smoke in its place. I studied it, squinting into the depths to try to make out an image.

Was that a figure? A woman, perhaps? And maybe some small spheres? I blinked, and it was gone.

"Any ideas?" I whispered at Cade.

"Shhhh!" Odin's loud hush made me wince.

Sorry! I didn't dare say it out loud.

The smoke died as quickly as it had appeared, and Frigg stepped around the basin and approached us.

Her eyes sparkled with something unrecognizable. "I cannot say I am entirely surprised by what I have seen."

"And what is that, wife?" Odin boomed.

She scowled at him, as if she thought little of the moniker, and said. "Idun."

"Ah." Odin clapped his hands. "Yes. This could very well be just what we have waited for."

"Idun?" I asked. "With the apples?"

"The very same." Frigg sat on the throne next to Odin. She looked at Cade, clearly attempting to clarify for him. "The goddess Idun tends the apples that keep us young. Without them, we will grow old and die."

Ah, and that explained their age. Something must have happened to Idun.

"She was kidnapped," Odin said. "We know not by whom, and all attempts to find her have been fruitless. Normally, I can see all from my great throne, Hliðskjálf. But I've seen nothing of her abduction."

"To prove that you are worthy of all the powers of the gods— to become the Master of Magic—you must do what the gods have failed to do. Rescue Idun."

Oh boy. "So you're saying I have a chance?"

"Yes," Frigg said. "Perhaps not a great one. It will be a trial in itself. A Viking hero's task that will test your mettle and determine if you are worthy. But if you succeed in saving Idun, Fate reveals that the rest of your powers will be delivered to you."

"When will I get my powers, exactly?"

"You forget yourself!" Odin bellowed.

I winced. He ran hot and cold, this one.

"I have good reason," I said. "I must—"

"I know, I know," he grumbled. He looked at Frigg. "What did the smoke say about this?"

"She will receive her powers when she returns Idun to our halls."

All right. That gave me some time. Not that I would delay in rescuing Idun—I didn't want her stuck with a kidnapper forever —but it would take me time to find her. In that time, hopefully Ana and Rowan could come up with a plan for ambushing the Rebel Gods. And it wasn't like they would attack me while I was in the realm of the Viking gods. They were too smart for that.

"I accept the challenge," I said.

Odin and Frigg nodded, each looking equally regal.

"Do you have any clues about where she is?" I asked.

"There is a rumor that she was taken by the son of a suitor of Greip."

"Greip?"

"A Jötunn," Odin said.

One of the giants. Though they weren't always giants in the traditional *huge* sense, from what I'd read. They were similar to gods, but with power over the natural elements rather than people. Many were large, but not all.

"Do you know anything else about her?" I asked.

"We do not," Odin said. "We can find no trace of her. It is like she never existed. I would consult the head of Mímir, but he has gone."

"Mímir was the wise man who lost his head in the Vanir-Aesir war?" I asked.

"The Aesir-Vanir war," Odin corrected. "And yes. He has been missing for over a year."

From the stories I'd read, Mímir had lost his head in the war, but he hadn't died. Odin had enchanted the head not to rot, and it provided wisdom to him. Without it, no wonder they had no leads on Idun's capture.

I bowed low, feeling a bit silly but it definitely seemed like an appropriate gesture. "I will find Idun."

"See that you do," Odin said. "For if you fail and we gods die of old age, you may never receive all your powers."

That would ensure the Rebel Gods wouldn't be able to use

their spell to find me, but I needed my powers to defeat them. I didn't want to be hunted for the rest of my life.

And the last thing I wanted to be responsible for was the death of all the Viking gods. Talk about *failure.*

So, yeah. We'd have to find Idun.

The golden-haired woman reappeared and escorted us from the room. Odin and Frigg's enormous magic faded as we departed the building, feeling like a weight lifting off my shoulders.

As the great golden doors shut behind us, Huginn and Muninn landed on the ground in front of us.

I looked at Cade. "Right. So we have to figure this out."

"We're looking for the son of a suitor of Greip."

"Except that as far as Odin is concerned, she doesn't exist." I frowned. "What if she isn't real? What if it's a kenning?"

"A kenning?"

"I read about it in my research. It's a poetic way of saying things for the Norse. A famous one is wound-hoe, which is a sword. A 'son of a suitor of Greip' could be just an obscure way to say a Jötunn. Since two Jötunn would make another Jötunn."

"Aye, I see. So it's not meant to point to a specific person."

"That's my best guess."

"Aye. So we should go to Jötunheimr, where most of them live?"

"You read my mind." I turned to the ravens. "Could one of you give us a ride to the entrance of Jötunheimr?"

The birds cawed, then grew twice their size. Three times. Soon, they were large enough to climb upon. I scrambled onto Huginn, and Cade climbed onto Muninn.

They took off into the air, rising high on the wind. Exhilaration filled me as the ravens flew over the city, then skimmed the treetops. They dived low and darted through a portal, appearing at the edge of Yggdrasil, high in the sky. The flight down made my stomach pitch. They flew for the roots of the tree like they were missiles plummeting downward.

I clung to them, desperate not to fall, as the wind tore at my hair and made my eyes water.

By the time we reached the bottom, I was panting, my arms aching. I tumbled off Huginn, then turned to thank him.

He cawed, pointing his beak toward a well set against the trunk of the tree. Huge boulders had tumbled around it.

The base of Yggdrasil was so wide that it was more like a cliff wall than a tree, large enough to support the formation of different mini ecosystems around it.

Like the pond where I'd sacrificed my sword, or this area of tumbled rocks.

When I looked at the well, a word flashed in my mind— *Mímisbrunnr.*

Huginn and Muninn took off toward the sky, flying out of sight. Their black feathers glinted in the light, and then they were gone.

I met Cade's gaze, then pointed to the well. "They wanted us to go over there, don't you think?"

"Aye."

I turned and started toward it, rolling the name *Mímisbrunnr* around in my head.

"Any reason this well is special?" Cade asked.

It was large and ancient, the stones worn smooth with time and set close to the trunk of Yggdrasil. Huge boulders towered around it. We stopped next to the well, and I peered into the depths to see nothing but blackness.

"A name flashed in my mind earlier," I said. "*Mímisbrunnr.* I think it means Mímir's well. Which would make this his well of wisdom."

"The one where Odin gave up his eye to drink from the waters."

"Ah, crap. Not the eye again." It'd been hard enough to let go of my sword. My eye would be too much.

I searched around the well, hoping for a clue of some kind. The ravens had been quite clear that we should come here. Did it have something to do with entering Jötunheimr?

Footprints in the dust caught my eye. They looked fairly fresh. But strange. One was a human footprint, the other a hoof. But they looked like they were standing together, both belonging to the same figure.

I stood up and searched the area around. The tumbled rocks around the well were large enough to hide someone.

"Hello?" I called.

No one responded, other than Cade. "Who are you calling for?"

I pointed to the footprints as I leaned against the well. "Someone was recently here." Mímir had gone missing from Odin recently. He was supposed to be just a head, but maybe... "Mímir? Is that you?"

Silence again.

Mímir would respect wisdom and cleverness. Therefore, if it was he who was hiding, I had to be clever. How would he have gotten here?

"Mímir, I think it is you who is hiding. This is your well, is it not? And there is a strange set of footprints."

"He has no feet," Cade said. "Do you think he got some more?"

"No one would want to live eternally, their head carried around by a grumpy old god. So I think that Mímir found some kind of magic to give himself a body. But it went a bit awry. He has a human leg and a goat's leg. There's no creature in Norse myth that has that. So I think it was created. Maybe by Mímir, since we are here at his well. And he mysteriously disappeared from Odin's grasp." I shrugged. "Or maybe he got someone to carry him."

"I can carry myself, thank you." A figure stepped out from behind a rock.

As expected, he had one human leg and one goat leg. The rest of him was human, save for the left arm that was actually a wing. His face looked pasty and strained.

"You are Mímir?" I asked. "I guessed correctly?"

He inclined his head. "I cannot say I am unimpressed."

Wow. It'd really felt like a shot in the dark, but I wasn't about to turn down a victory. "So you did run away from Odin."

"Of course. It took me centuries to find a way to build myself a body, but I am not called the wisest man for nothing."

"Yet Odin hasn't searched for you here?" Cade asked.

I had to agree. It seemed pretty obvious.

"He has, but I avoid him. He doesn't own me. No one does. But he kept me prisoner for years, using my knowledge for his own. He may have drunk from the well of knowledge, but *I* am the expert."

Odin might be called the Allfather, but he wasn't always paternalistic, from what I'd read. He could be quite ruthless. And this just went to prove it.

"So you've returned here to drink from the well," I said. "To regain your knowledge."

A splash sounded from inside the well, and I turned. Though I peered hard into the blackness, I saw nothing.

I turned back to Mímir to find him watching me closely. "Fish?"

"Yes." He gave us a hard look. "Now, why are you here?"

"We are looking for Idun, and the ravens pointed us in this direction."

"Huginn and Muninn?" he asked.

"The same. Why did they help me?"

"They are wise as well. Perhaps they saw that you are worthy. You are the Valkyrie Dragon God, are you not?"

"I am. Can you tell us anything about Idun? Have you heard about her abduction?"

"Perhaps. But you must answer a riddle first."

I stifled a groan. "Does it have to be a riddle?"

"I'm bored. Riddles entertain me. But perhaps you can have a historical riddle. If you know your history, it will be easy to answer."

I kind of knew my history. At least, I'd been reading up on the Vikings in every spare moment. "Fine. What is it?"

"Logi and Loki once held an eating contest. Which one was the victor?"

I definitely knew who Loki was. But Logi?

Mímir watched us with a crafty gleam in his eyes as I leaned toward Cade.

"Ever heard of Logi?" I asked.

"No."

I looked at Mímir. "One hint. Who is Logi?"

"I can tell you, but you'll have to tell me *why* your chosen one was the winner."

"Fine."

Mímir smiled. "Logi is a fire spirit."

Hmmm. I looked at Cade, head spinning. "It can't be that Logi burned all the food. That's not eating it."

"Loki has many tricks up his sleeve. Always. He could turn himself into a giant to eat as much as he wanted."

"True." But something was tugging me toward Logi. Then it clicked. "Fire consumes everything. That's it! Loki can eat endlessly, but fire consumes everything. Logi probably ate the plate and even the table as well."

Mímir smiled. "Well done, indeed."

"So we succeeded? You'll tell me what you know about the abduction of Idun and her apples?"

"I have heard that she was taken by a Jötunn. Likely to Jötunheimr. More specifically, in Utgard. The Jötunn Thjazi once took her. They have done so again, I believe."

It confirmed what we'd interpreted from Odin's gossip. One more thing pointing us in the direction of Jötunheimr.

"How do we get to Jötunheimr? It must be near here, because we asked the ravens to bring us to the entrance."

"You are correct." He pointed to the massive root that wound around the great rocks. "That root connects this plane to Jötunheimr. Step upon it, and it will carry you up."

Well, that was weird. But I was talking to a guy who was part human, part goat, and part bird, so nothing was very normal today.

"Is there anything we should be aware of in Jötunheimr?" Cade asked.

"Everything." The expression on Mímir's face made me shiver. "But in particular, the cold and the ire of the giants. You should seek the palace at Utgard, but avoid the giants."

"Utgard?" I frowned. "Does that have anything to do with the concept of utangard?"

"Indeed it does. You will be well outside of the realm of inangard. Utgard and Jötunheimr are centers of utangard."

I grimaced. Of course this wouldn't be easy.

Mímir gestured to the root. "Go on now. I have things to be doing." With that, he turned and walked off.

"What's this about utangard and inangard?" Cade asked.

"They're the Norse concepts for safe and unsafe, essentially. Asgard is a place of inangard—so are villages and homes. They are places within the bounds of law and rightness. Utangard is the opposite. Lawless and dangerous."

"Just our kind of place, then."

"Exactly." I walked up to the root that grew out of the ground. It was massive, I realized. A large flat platform that burst out of the earth and then dived back into it.

I scrambled onto it, Cade at my side. As soon as we reached the top, magic fizzled around us. Then the root burst from the earth, plunging upward.

Fear froze my skin, but I didn't fall off the root and plummet to my death like I expected. The magic had gotten ahold of me and carried me along. Faster and faster we shot through the sky, heading for the leaves high above.

When we plunged into darkness, my head spun. I gasped, trying to get my bearings, but it was impossible when riding a magical tree root up to the top of the universe.

The ride stopped abruptly, and I tumbled off the platform. Cade rolled off along with me.

I scrambled to my feet, cold slicing through my bones, and looked upon a barren hellscape of icy misery.

9

"Ah, excellent. Just what I was hoping for." I shivered, making a mockery of my statement.

The landscape stretching out before us was barren and gray. Snow flurried though the air, whipping past huge trees that put the giant redwoods to shame. These were the trees of giants. Not Yggdrasil—nothing was like that tree—but these were the size of New York City skyscrapers. The river to our left was massively wide, tumbling gray and icy over boulders and downed tree limbs.

"Given your explanation of utangard, it's roughly what I would expect," Cade said.

"Yes, though looking at the place, I wish that Mímir had recommended we go another direction to find Idun."

"Aye, he was an odd sort."

"Wasn't he though?" I huddled farther into my jacket, studying the terrain. Which way to go?

A massive collection of icy boulders caught my eye. They were a couple hundred yards in the distance, but there was something strange about them.

It was as good a lead as any. "Come on."

We hurried through the cold, keeping our strides long and our heads bowed against the wind. As we neared the boulders that towered forty feet overhead, I realized that they were mostly ice rather than rock. And they were a vaguely familiar shape.

When the icy mass moved, I stumbled backward, heart jumping. Cade went on high alert, drawing his sword. I started to, realizing too late that I'd sacrificed my sword. I drew my daggers instead, feeling woefully underprepared.

The massive creature that rose to four feet made my muscles turn to jelly.

"Oh, this is bad," I muttered.

It was a fox. Or a wolf. Hard to tell, considering that it was made of ice and stone. Cold eyes peered at us.

I glanced at Cade and whispered, "Get ready to shift and run if you have to."

"You'll fly?"

I nodded, keeping one eye on the fox.

Yep—it was definitely a fox. It'd be cute, if it weren't massive and fangy. Long icicle-like fangs extended from its mouth. Being impaled on one had to be the absolute worst way to go.

It lowered its head to sniff us, going first for me, then for Cade. Though my flight or fight reflex begged to do either of those very fine options, I held perfectly still.

The fox's eyes might be cold, but I didn't immediately sense danger from him. And the fight option was actually terrible. Poking this enormous ice fox with my dagger would definitely get me chomped in half.

"Who are you?" The fox's voice was deep and strong.

So that's what the fox says.

Except I couldn't even laugh at my own inane joke. "I'm Bree Blackwood, the Valkyrie Dragon God."

"I am Belatucadros," Cade said.

The fox's icy gaze landed on me. "You, I know." His gaze

drifted to Cade, and he sniffed him again. "You are a god. A wolf."

"Sometimes."

The fox huffed, his back legs shifting, and little ice chips fell off him.

"What are you doing here, tiny food?" he asked.

Ah, shit. Tiny food. That was us.

"We're here to find Idun, the goddess with the apples of youth," I said. "Have you seen her?"

Interest gleamed in the fox's eyes. "I see all in this realm, and no, I have not seen her."

Dang. "We're trying to get to the fortress city of Utgard. We were told that she may have been abducted to that place."

"Told by whom?" The fox licked his lips with an icy tongue.

I swallowed hard. "Mímir, the wise man."

"Do not trust all wise men. Not all wisdom is truth."

I didn't know what to make of that, but it did sound smart. "Could you tell us where Utgard is?"

"Perhaps I would prefer to eat you," the fox said. "You are tiny and bony, but would make a good snack."

"I can see how it would seem that way." I got ready to call upon my wings, hoping that Cade would be prepared to run. "But we're actually very tough. Our muscles make us stringy."

The fox looked thoughtful. "I don't like stringy meat."

"Who does?"

Next to me, Cade huffed a laugh so quiet I might have imagined it.

"So maybe you could tell us where to go?" I asked.

The fox sighed. "Perhaps I could. But what would you do for me in exchange?"

"What do you want?"

"I have a few things in mind." He sat on his haunches. "But

the most important one is that I would like an apple from Idun's basket."

"You're ice and stone though. Could the apple really work on you?"

"Not for immortality. But it would make me stronger. The apples are immensely valuable." Greed shined in his eyes, and suddenly, I realized that he'd been leading into this. He'd wanted the apple all along—not a tiny bony snack, as he'd said.

I had to wonder if Odin even cared about Idun for her own sake. It was probably just the apples. And this fox really wanted one, too.

"I can promise to ask Idun for you," I said. "But I can't promise that she will deliver."

"I want a promise," the fox bellowed.

I winced as his icy breath flew over me. "I'll tell her how much you helped us save her. I'll even make it sound like it was impossible without you."

"It *will* be impossible if I decide to eat you."

I blanched. "That's a fair point. But I promise, I will do everything in my power to get you an apple."

The fox looked toward Cade.

Cade nodded his head once. "On my honor."

"Good." The fox turned to point his nose toward the roaring river. "If you follow the water downstream, it will lead you to a clearing. Continue to follow, and eventually you will come across Utgard."

"How will we know it is the proper place?" Cade asked.

The fox laughed, a strange, rusty sound. "Oh, you will know. There is no fortress like it. But breaking in may be nearly impossible."

"We'll manage," I said. "And we'll make sure you receive an apple."

"Beware of Utgard-Loki's games. He is smart and powerful, and you will not win."

"Utgard-Loki?" Cade asked.

"The trickster of the Jötunn. Beware of him."

I thought I recognized the name from my research, but I didn't recall much else.

"We'll be wary," I said.

The fox settled back down and stared at us. "You should go now."

I saluted. "Thank you for the help."

Cade duplicated my thanks, and we both spun and hurried away toward the river.

I could feel the fox's gaze burning into my back as we strode away. It might have been made of ice, but it sure was hot.

"I think this realm is going to be trouble," Cade said.

"Agreed." I reached the edge of the river and turned to head downstream.

The water smelled fresh and icy, and it splashed and swirled as it traveled over the rocks dotted through the river. It had to be ten miles across, at least. Silver fish jumped within, each the size of a whale, but with gleaming white fangs. It was nearly impossible to keep my eyes off of them.

We walked as quickly as we could, as much to keep warm as for the sake of speed.

As we walked, I touched my comms charm to ignite the magic. It was a cool and handy device, courtesy of the Protectorate, and I could get used to it.

"Ana? Rowan?" I asked.

"Hey!" Ana's voice crackled through. "Where are you? Have any luck?"

"I'm in Jötunheimr, and no luck yet, but we're on the trail. What about you? Have you found the crystals?"

"Not yet, but we're close," Ana said.

"Is Rowan there? Is she okay?"

"She's in the other room. She's fine. But her magic is still broken. She's... having a slightly hard time."

"To be expected." But it still made my heart ache. "Well, good luck with it. I'm going to go and focus on not getting killed."

"I should do some of that myself. Good luck. Love you."

"Love you back." I glanced at Cade.

I loved him, too. No question.

But now was not the time to share that tidbit.

A harsh screech rent the air, sending ice through my veins. I flinched and looked up, searching the sky. The leafless canopy was far above, the skeletal branches of the trees shrouded in clouds.

"Can you see it?" I asked.

"Nothing." He squinted upward. "I think it's far ahead of us and above the clouds."

"So, in the same direction that we're headed?"

"Aye."

"Perfect. The giant fox wasn't scary enough."

He chuckled.

We trooped along in silence, our footsteps crunching on the icy ground. My jacket wasn't doing much to keep me warm, and Cade's sweater didn't look much better. But as long as we kept moving, we'd be okay.

"Fates, I hope Idun is still alive," I said. "Being trapped in this realm would be awful."

"They need her for her apples. They wouldn't kill her."

He was likely right, and I clung to his words.

The screeching noise continued intermittently as we ran.

"My guess is giant bird." I panted.

"If he's anything like that fox, I'd prefer not to meet him."

I grinned.

By the time we reached the edge of the forest, my feet were pretty numb. I'd have to do some serious healing soon, but I'd save my energy for now.

The field in front of us was barren. Maybe once it had grown crops, but now, it was a flat expanse of nothing.

I shivered. "We'll be exposed out there."

"Too exposed."

I reached for his hand. When his warm fingers closed around mine, heat shot up my arm. In this chill weather, I could use a lot more than that.

As I used Loki's power to make us invisible, I wondered what Utgard-Loki would be like. I did *not* want to meet the trickster Jötunn if I could help it. No thanks.

We started across the field at a slow jog, following the massive river that cut through the middle. When a large shape swooped down from the clouds, my steps faltered.

Holy fates, that was a big eagle.

"Cade."

"I see it."

The thing had to be the size of a 747. Every time it flapped its wings, a massive burst of wind blew my hair back and stung my cheeks. Worse, the eagle began to circle us. Like a vulture.

"I don't like what he's doing," I said.

The eagle dived low, right in front of us. My heart jumped into my throat.

"I like this even less," Cade said.

The eagle landed ten feet away, his massive claws pounding onto the earth and shaking the ground all the way up to my teeth.

"Who goes there?" the eagle demanded. His voice was a terrifying screech that sent shudders across my skin. He was so tall that I had to crane my head back to see him, and his beady eyes watched me with interest.

I looked at Cade, but he was still invisible.

"I can smell you, invisible ones."

Whelp, the jig was up. And no way we could outrun him. The fox, maybe. A giant wind-creating eagle? Nope.

"Birds can smell?" I asked.

"I can! I'm no ordinary bird. I am Corpse Swallower."

Shit. That rang a bell. Corpse Swallower was a giant eagle that ate corpses and made the wind with its wings.

"You are the great and mighty Hraesvelgr?" I asked, deciding that flattery was my safest bet.

"Of course I am. And what are you?"

I squeezed Cade's hand, then dropped the illusion, leaving him hidden but revealing myself. "I am Bree Blackwood, the Valkyrie Dragon God."

The eagle whistled through its beak. "Are you really? And who is your invisible friend?"

So much for protecting Cade. I dropped the illusion from him.

"I am Belatucadros," he said.

"Ah, the War Wolf. I have seen you from the sky. You fight well, War Wolf."

Cade inclined his head. "Thank you, Great Hraesvelgr."

His pronunciation was a little off, but the eagle ruffled his feathers, clearly liking the term "Great".

"I hope you're not going to eat us," I said.

"If you die, perhaps. I don't do the killing—just the eating. Though you look tiny and bony. What are you doing here, tiny bony ones?"

"You aren't the first one to call us tiny and bony."

"The fox?" Hraesvelgr said. "That interloping, no-good, egg-sucking son of a rat."

I didn't think the fox was quite *that* bad, but I didn't want to get in the middle of a Norse monster grudge-fest. I'd leave that to Ratatoskr.

"We are seeking Idun," I said. "You must see everything from up there in the sky. Have you seen her?"

"I have not. But would that I had." The eagle's gaze took on a faraway cast. "Her apples are the most coveted in the land."

Everyone wanted a piece of those apples.

"We've been told that she may have been abducted to Utgard," Cade said. "Is it near here?"

"It doesn't matter," the eagle said. "Even if she were there, and it were near, you couldn't get in. You cannot fly."

"I can," I said.

He huffed. "Well, of course you can, Valkyrie. But the wolf cannot."

"He can run up walls and jump higher than you've ever seen."

The eagle screeched a laugh. "Not over the walls of Utgard!" I thought he would roll over with laughter. "What an idea!"

"Can you tell us how to get in, then? Or perhaps give us a ride?"

His laughter died abruptly. "A ride?!"

"Um, I mean. Of course not! But perhaps there is a way in? Or some advice you can give us?"

He frowned at me—it should have been impossible, given that he had a beak and not lips, but he *definitely* made a thoughtful frowny face. "Perhaps I could. But only if you swear to me to bring me one of Idun's apples."

"Really?" Man, these apples were popular. "Do you need more strength? I know you're not dead."

"Of course not. Do I look like I need more strength?" He stretched his wings wide, and they cast us in shadow. He was wider than a city block, and sent ice through my veins. This eagle could chomp me down in one gulp.

"Of course you don't need more strength!" I said. "But I assumed, since you also don't need more life, correct?"

"Correct. But I have a friend whose health is flagging. It will help him."

Well, that was reasonable. "I promise that I will beg Idun on your behalf. I cannot make any promises, as her apples are not my own, but I will try."

The eagle gave me a keen look. "I like your answer. It's honest. What of you, War Wolf?"

"I vow to help her."

The eagle nodded. "See to it that you uphold your end of the bargain. I will come after you if you fail to convince Idun." He snapped his beak. "You will not like it."

I winced, getting the feeling that he would bend his corpses-only rule. "I swear, we will."

Actually, I wasn't even sure we *could* convince Idun. But that was a problem for another time.

The eagle stared at us, turning his head so he could pin us with one beady eye. It was like he was trying to put all of his creep factor into that one single glare. He was laser focusing it on us by shooting it through one eye.

It worked, because I shivered. Finally, though, I had to say something. "We can't get you an apple until you tell us how to get into Utgard."

He stared for a few seconds more. "Just making sure I put the fear of Hraesvelgr into you."

"Don't worry. I feel it." The words felt silly, but the shaking in my legs didn't. I was going to have to work hard to convince Idun, because I did not want this eagle on my tail.

"I heard the funeral song today," Hraesvelgr said. "They bury their dead outside Utgard's walls—to the east."

I didn't need to ask how he knew that, given his choice of food.

"If you hurry, you can find the Jötunn at the graveside. Use your invisibility and follow them back into Utgard."

"Which way is east?" This wasn't earth, and I could see no sun to guide us.

The eagle jerked his beak over his right shoulder. "That way. You are currently heading north."

"Thank you."

"But I warn you!" he said. "Do not play the trickster's games. Do not let him even see you."

"Utgard-Loki?" Cade asked.

"The very same." Hraesvelgr turned his head again. "Now, do not forget your end of the bargain! Or I will hunt you to the ends of Yggdrasil."

I gulped and nodded, believing everything he said.

Then he took off, powerful wings carrying him high into the sky. The blast of wind blew me off my feet, sending me slamming onto the ground. Cade crashed down next to me.

Pain flared through my tailbone, and I flopped down onto my back, watching the enormous eagle fly into the clouds.

"There sure are a lot of giant animals in this realm," I muttered.

Cade groaned. "I think I prefer Ratatoskr."

"At least he's just a moody gossip." Aching, I climbed to my feet.

Cade joined me, and we set off, running northeast, toward Utgard. I used Loki's power to conceal us from any other watchers—though I doubted its power if our enemy had a good sense of smell—and we held hands to keep track of each other.

After a while, dread began to curl in my stomach. There was nothing but white mist ahead of us, and we'd been running for ages. Had we missed it? Was it impossibly far?

Then my eyes focused on it.

The mist was not mist at all. It was solid ice. I squinted, using Heimdall's power, and the ice began to reveal details.

It was a wall.

I tilted my head back, trying to see to the top.

And I couldn't.

"Crap, Cade. Do you see that?"

"The castle that is as big as a planet? Because aye, I do."

"I don't think it's a castle, exactly." I craned my neck to take in either side of the thing. "It's a walled city."

"We could run through the corridors like mice. If the Jötunn are truly large enough to make that their home, we won't have a chance against them. Not in a fight."

"The mouse plan is a good one." I'd pretend to be a rodent to avoid meeting a hostile being who was that big. "Come on."

We turned right, heading toward the east and keeping at least two miles between the city walls and us. As we ran, I began to pick up the faint sound of wailing. It had a melodic quality—some kind of funeral dirge.

I picked up the pace. "We're getting closer."

"I hear it."

By the time we'd skirted around part of the city and caught sight of the funeral, I had no breath left to spare. I managed a gasp, however, at the sight of the Jötunn.

Most of them were, in fact, giants. There were blue ones made of ice, and others who looked more like huge humans. A few smaller individuals milled around their feet, but they only went up to the giants' ankles. All of them wore ancient Norse clothing—cloaks and furs, accented with gold and silver.

Cade and I slowed to a halt, taking it in. There were at least fifty of them, all gathered around a mound of earth. Who had been strong enough to dig a grave in this frozen ground?

I supposed that was the least of my worries.

I watched as they finished the funeral, my interest piqued

but my heart thundering. I caught snippets of words, but didn't understand much. The songs sounded depressing as hell, though. Perfect for a funeral.

As they turned to go back to the castle, I squeezed Cade's hand.

This was our moment.

We followed them closely, keeping our footsteps silent as we approached a huge gate set into the wall. Up close, I realized that the icy castle wall was mixed with stone—almost like a weird concrete. The enormous gate creaked open, and the Jötunn filed through. We followed, hurrying to keep ahead of the last giant.

It took some fancy footwork to avoid being squished beneath a huge boot, but we managed. As we crossed under the gate, a frisson of magic streaked across my skin.

Oh, shit.

It was some kind of protective charm.

Cade's hand tightened on mine, his own version of cursing.

Before I had a chance to decide if we should lunge into the city or back out, the Jötunn turned to look at us, their massive faces peering down.

Only then did I realize that our invisibility was gone.

The protective charm.

Just our luck. Their city gates were fortified against invisibility.

The massive gate slammed down behind us, trapping us within the city of giants.

We were screwed.

10

I stared up at the giants, panicky ideas racing through my head.

I could fly away, but that would leave Cade unable to escape. I could....

Yeah, that was my only idea. And it was crap.

"Go," he hissed, dropping my hand.

As if.

"Not going anywhere."

"We're screwed if we're both captured."

"We've broken out of plenty of places before. And I'm not leaving you." Not when I'd just realized I loved him. And also because it would be freaking cowardly and miserable.

One of the giants stepped forward, glaring down at us with an angry face that looked like a cross between a pug and a human. But cleverness lurked in his dark eyes. He wore rough clothing made of animal skins—but what animal was big enough to clothe a giant?

I really didn't want to find out.

"Why do you invade during our time of grief?" he demanded.

Oh, shit. How the heck was I supposed to answer that?

None of my answers sounded good, and did I really want to reveal our motives? No.

We needed to buy time until we could sneak away and find Idun.

"I wanted to see the greatness of Utgard-Loki." I almost winced. That sounded totally ridiculous. Who would buy that? But the giant straightened, reminding me of Boris when I'd complimented him. *Play to his pride.* "I see that you are even more impressive than I expected."

"Of course I am." He frowned. "Now tell me why you are really here."

Dang. But at least I now knew he was Utgard-Loki. The one we were supposed to avoid at all costs.

"We seek answers." My mind raced. "Someone—um, not you—has abducted Idun. The goddess with the apples of immortality."

"Not us?" His brow lowered. "You sound like you are, in fact, accusing us."

"No!" I held up my hands, placating. "Of course not! But we were advised to come here to seek our answers. That you might have...someone to help us find her. Or direct us toward her."

A murmur went through the crowd of giants. Clearly annoyed. Offended, even.

"You think to impose upon our hospitality?" Utgard-Loki said. "You sneak in here and think to steal information from us?"

"Of course not!"

He scowled, his heavy brow drawing low over his eyes. He snapped a finger at someone behind us.

I turned and looked up, just in time to see a massive hand come down. I nearly peed my pants, but the hand just pinched the back of my jacket and lifted me up. I swung in the air, rising higher and higher. A hundred feet up.

Holy fates!

I froze. *Don't drop me!*

I wouldn't be able to unfurl my wings before I hit the ground. The giant dipped his other hand down, snatching up Cade. He appeared at my side as we both dangled in front of the giant's chest.

"Well, this is undignified," Cade said.

Terrified laughter collided inside me. "This is not how I expected to go."

"You're not going anywhere yet." Utgard-Loki flicked his fingers. "Come. Bring them to the great hall."

My jacket cut into my armpits as the giant carried us through the massive courtyard and into a huge entry hall. If I lived to tell the tale of this, I was going to run out of words to describe a place this huge. I needed to read *Gulliver's Travels,* but from the Lilliputian perspective.

"If you break free, can you use your wings to save yourself?" Cade whispered.

"No. And I'm not leaving you." I knew we would find answers here. Maybe even Idun.

And I wasn't going to ditch him. Not now, not ever.

We rode along with the procession of giants, entering a banquet hall with a fireplace as big as the whole Protectorate castle. The flames flickered high and huge, looking like the gates to hell.

I averted my gaze, following Utgard-Loki to the main table. He sat in an enormous throne carved of wood—no doubt from the huge trees we'd seen in the forest. How was Odin the famous one when these guys existed?

The giant who carried us dropped us on the table in front of Utgard-Loki, and my skin chilled.

"I really feel like dinner down here," I said.

"At least we're not on plates." Cade gave me a hard look. "Fly out of here."

"No." I swallowed hard and looked up at Utgard-Loki.

"Who are you?" he demanded.

The giants who had seated themselves around him turned their heads to stare at us.

"I am Bree Blackwood, the Valkyrie Dragon god."

"I am Belatucadros," Cade said.

We'd really spent *way* too much time today introducing ourselves to massive creatures that could destroy us.

Utgard-Loki stared hard at us, then turned and bellowed. "Syn!"

I waited, breathless, until finally, I could hear someone enter the room. Her footsteps sounded light. Like she was human. Or human-sized, at least. I tilted my head to hear better. Sounded like she was nearing the table. Then there was a crackle of magic, and a person grew up from the floor.

I saw her head first, appearing at the edge of the table. She continued to grow until she was the size of one of the giants, but it was magic rather than nature.

She had long blonde hair and blue eyes, and her magic was that of a god's. It rolled over me, strong and fierce, feeling like clarity of mind and hard steel pressed against my throat.

I swallowed hard and met her gaze.

Syn, he'd called her. That would make her the goddess of truth.

I could definitely make use of a power like hers.

"Why do you call me, Utgard-Loki?" Her voice resonated with power.

He pointed to us. "Are they who they say they are?"

She stared hard at us, blue eyes glinting. "And who are you?"

We repeated the introductions.

"Truth," she said.

"Humph." Utgard-Loki crossed his arms over his chest. "Why are you here?"

"We seek to right a wrong, not cause any harm to you." It was true, but would it satisfy them?

"Truth," Syn said. "But which wrong?"

"The abduction of Idun."

Syn frowned. "Hmm."

Utgard-Loki dipped down until his head was level with mine. "Interesting." He sniffed, trying to get a sense of my magic. "If you aren't here to cause us harm, but require our help"—*I wasn't sure I'd go that far*—"then I think this calls for a challenge."

"A challenge?"

"Yes. Traditional." He grinned. "Also entertaining."

"What is the challenge?"

"It will be a traditional hero's challenge. If you accomplish the tasks laid out for you, we will allow you to ask three questions of Syn to help you in your task." He looked at her for confirmation, and she nodded. "If you fail, however, you become dinner."

Shit.

Right, so we didn't want to fail.

But succeeding could help us find Idun. Syn's guidance could come in very handy. If only she'd give me some of her power. Since I didn't think that would happen anytime soon, this was our best option.

Our only option, since they could squish us like bugs in a heartbeat.

I glanced at Cade, who nodded.

Hero's challenge it was, then.

Which wasn't dissimilar to what Frigg had said we would face.

"What is our challenge to be?" I asked.

Utgard-Loki leaned back in his chair, a delighted expression on his face. "It will be for someone your size, of course, and begin with a race. Then a strength challenge, then a fight."

Cade and I could do all of those things. "All right. Let's start."

Someone grabbed the back of my jacket again, hoisting me into the air. My stomach plummeted as I swung two hundred feet above the ground. Out of the corner of my eye, I could spot Cade, swinging just like I was.

They carried us out of the great hall and into the courtyard. We rode along for what felt like ages, never leaving the walls of the city.

I took the opportunity to use my healing magic to fix my frozen toes. They were probably a bit frostbitten, which would do me no favors in a race. Then I pressed my fingertips to my comms charm, whispering into it, "Ana, Rowan. Any luck with the crystals?"

"Almost," Ana whispered back, mimicking my tone.

"Good. Keep going."

"Good luck there."

"Thanks." I would need it.

When we neared a tiny forest, I frowned.

They had human-sized places here?

I caught sight of a cabin in the woods—a creepy old cottage that looked haunted as hell. Then the giants put us on the ground at the edge of the forest, and I lost sight of it.

From above, Utgard-Loki's voice boomed. "You will race to the cottage, where you will pick up the cat. Be careful to choose the correct cat, or you will forfeit your life. Pick up the cat, then the fight will begin."

What the heck? I leaned toward Cade and whispered, "Talk about some properly weird mythological challenges."

"That's the truth, and you don't need Syn to confirm it."

Many of the old stories I'd read had been similarly strange. But *pick up the cat?*

What the heck?

A man appeared at our side, small and slight. "Ready to run?"

I looked at him, taking in his short stature and even shorter legs. "Are you our competition?"

"That I am." He grinned and shook his blond hair off his forehead.

We had a shot against a guy of his stature, definitely. I sucked in a deep breath, glancing at Cade. He nodded.

"Yes, we're ready."

The man pointed down the path. "That will lead to the cottage. First one there, wins."

I could do that. "Can I fly?"

He grinned. "Sure. It won't help you, but sure."

We'd see about that. I hiked a thumb at Cade. "Can he shift into a wolf?"

"All right." The man chuckled.

Competitive fire rose in my chest. I wasn't going to let this chuckling lunatic beat me. Hell no. Not just for Idun. For my honor—what there was of it, at least.

I stretched, looking up at Utgard-Loki, who loomed so far overhead that he could have been a mountain. "Will you call it?"

He nodded. The giants around him rustled, clearly getting excited.

Cade and I got into a running stance. I wouldn't fly unless I had to, and he seemed to be of the same mind about shifting.

Utgard-Loki cleared his throat. "Three, two, one."

At one, I sprinted ahead, Cade at my side.

Our competitor raced forward.

We ran, side by side. Air heaved in my lungs as I pushed

myself, muscles aching. But the man pulled ahead. His short legs seemed to do him no harm at all.

"Damn it," Cade growled. Magic swirled around him, golden and bright, and he shifted into his wolf form.

I called on my wings, feeling them unfurl from my back, and took to the sky. I pushed myself upward, but not so high that I lost any time on vertical gains.

My new speed was faster, and I shot forward, zipping down the path. Below, Cade raced in his wolf form. His huge paws ate up the ground, and he gained on the man.

Then the man stopped, and turned. He ran back toward Cade. Did a circle around him.

What the heck!

He was just showing off.

I flew faster, and he didn't seem to notice me as I passed overhead. He was busy running circles around Cade, who was clearly pissed, his muzzle drawn back from his fangs as he sprinted along.

Though I'd been able to see the cottage from above when I'd been held in the giant's grip, I was too low and far away right now.

But I kept flying, trying to put as much distance as possible between the man and me.

A shout sounded from behind me.

He'd seen me!

I pushed myself faster, but soon, he was sprinting along underneath me, taking the lead.

Frustration burned in my chest as my head pounded. Oxygen was in short supply in my body, and everything ached.

Without warning, the path cut off, running into a wall of water that appeared out of nowhere. It rose hundreds of feet high, clear and blue, sparkling in the sun. I could see straight through it, making out trees and rocks and even the path.

It was not a true body of water, else it'd be full of seaweed and fish. Instead, it was just plopped down on land.

I'd have thought that it was trickery on the Jötunn's part, meant to slow me, but my opponent had to deal with it, too.

He plowed right into the sparkling liquid, slowing as he became surrounded, but he continued to run on the path.

Not swim—*run.*

That should've been impossible.

I looked up. Could I fly over?

Eventually, maybe. But it'd take time, and it would leave Cade behind. We were strongest as a pair. I wouldn't be the one to break that.

I called on my water magic, feeling the heavy liquid deep in my body, like it was part of me. Maybe this was part of the challenge—to use the magic the gods had gifted me.

It only made sense, for a hero's challenge.

That way, I could become the Master of my Magic and earn my victory.

It took every bit of magic I had to part the water. For some reason, it was more difficult than normal. My breath heaved as I gave it everything I had, eventually splitting the water to reveal the sodden path.

I made sure not to clear the way for our opponent, who was still ahead of us, and flew between the walls of water.

Below, Cade caught up, racing on the muddy path, flinging dark droplets up behind him. I panted as I flew, trying to keep the water away from us. It pressed in on me, as if the goddess Rán herself was fighting me.

Every muscle in my body ached as I fought my way through, holding back the water.

Twenty feet ahead of us, our opponent burst out of the water and onto the cleared path. My magic split the rest of the water.

Almost there.

I raced toward it, Cade putting on a blast of extra speed.

I was shaking by the time I flew out of my water tunnel and dropped my control immediately. Nothing happened—nothing but dead silence.

I glanced backward to see the water hadn't crashed back together—it'd just disappeared.

Oh, I don't like that.

I turned back and flew harder, trying to keep up with the man who was now leaving us in the dust without the water to slow his way.

When the first lightning bolt struck, I nearly jumped out of my skin, faltering on the air. It pierced a tree to my left, sending smoke rising into the sky.

Another bolt struck the path in front of us—only feet from Cade's muzzle.

Shit!

Another challenge.

Another one that related to my magic.

I called on Thor's power, trying to feel the lightning in the sky. Soon, there was a crackle and burn in my chest. It connected me to the clouds, helping me feel where the lightning was forming.

A bolt plowed out of the sky and struck our competitor in the head.

He shook and stumbled, going briefly to his knees, but didn't seem overly bothered. What the hell? We used the few seconds advantage to catch up, but he was on his feet soon, still racing ahead of us.

I focused on the crackle of energy in the air and in my chest, feeling where the lightning would strike next. When it plunged from the sky, headed right for me, I darted left, trying to grab the lightning's electrical energy and divert it away.

It worked—kind of—striking a nearby branch instead of me.

The light was so close and so bright that it temporarily blinded me, and my eardrums were probably bleeding from the crack of thunder.

Oh, shit.

I shook my head and blinked, vision coming back in flashes. A tree appeared in front of me, and I swerved just in time.

Lightning crackled in my chest again, right before it struck. It nearly plowed into Cade, but I caught it just in time, reaching out with my magic like it was an extension of me. A third hand able to grab the lightning and hurl it away from Cade.

Power flowed through me as I heaved the lightning away, forcing it to strike a tree instead of the man I loved.

Wow.

Was this what Thor felt? True control over the lightning?

It was *amazing.*

The rest of the bolts were easier—I could sense them sooner each time and grab them quicker. Soon, I quit sending the bolts at the trees. Instead, I directed them toward the path in front of our opponent, forcing him to dodge and dive.

I never sent them straight at him—there was no way to tell if he was a prisoner like us. Even with so much at stake, I couldn't just light up an innocent man, electrocuting him. That was no way to win.

Anyway, this was working well. He had to dodge so many bolts that we were catching up, gaining on him with every step.

By the time I spotted the cottage up ahead, we were nearly to him.

Then, the lightning stopped coming.

The man sprinted ahead.

Oh, hell no.

I called on the lightning, trying to conjure more to distract him, but he was so fast that he reached the house in seconds, leaving us in the dust.

He was so fast I could hardly see him.

Holy crap, had he been holding back all this time?

Frustrated rage welled in my chest.

We'd lost.

And something felt totally off about it. Maybe I was a sore loser—it was possible—but I still didn't like it. This felt like a trick.

Cade loped up to the house, joining the man just as I landed.

The man turned and grinned at me, looking as refreshed as he had the moment we'd started the race. In contrast, I heaved like an old car trying to make it up a hill, sweat pouring down my face and my muscles aching.

"That was nice!" the man said.

"*Nice?*" I wanted to punch him.

In a swirl of gold, Cade shifted back to human. He was red-faced, too, and his scowl was just as strong as mine. Neither of us was used to losing, and we definitely didn't like it.

"Who are you?" I panted.

"Hugi." He smiled again.

The name was familiar, but I couldn't grasp it. "What is your magic?"

"Enough!" Utgard-Loki bellowed. "Be gone, Hugi."

Hugi nodded and scampered off, zipping back down the path like he'd never run it in the first place.

Panting, I turned to Cade. "That was weird, right? Like he was holding back the whole time, then bam! So fast it hardly seems possible."

He nodded, opening his mouth to answer, but Utgard-Loki cut him off. "Enter! And choose *wisely.*"

I looked up, wanting to ask if he meant *pick up the cat* in the literal sense, but the door to the cottage swung open and a massive finger poked me in the back, shoving me through.

My wings barely fit, and I lost some feathers on the way. I retracted them into my body, studying the house I'd entered.

Cats sat on every surface, each with gleaming fur and bright eyes. Orange, black, yellow, white, brown. Even a blue one.

"Holy shite," Cade muttered.

He'd been pushed in, too, and stood next to me, jaw hanging open.

The room was large, and I could see bits of other rooms as well, doorways leading to more spacious areas cluttered with furniture and cats.

So many cats.

11

"They really meant I have to pick up a cat," I said.

"Aye." Bewilderment filled Cade's voice.

"Myths are weird."

"Aye. And this is the weirdest."

"That's how we know it's legit, at least."

I studied the room and the cats. The space was entirely done up for their pleasure. Cat beds rested on every surface, and fancy wooden towers reached for the ceiling, giving the animals a place to climb. Windows were open so the cats could go outside, but most seemed content to stay within the house.

Fortunately, there was no scent of cat litter. They must make use of the great outdoors.

"If I was ever going to become a cat lady, I'd want to do it like this," I said.

"They do look happy."

A hundred pairs of eyes stared at me, all different colors. "How do I choose? It can't be just any cat. That's too easy."

"Aye, that'll be part of the challenge. Pick up the proper cat."

"The proper cat," I muttered, strolling through the entry room and into a living room.

There were more cats. Still more in the dining room and library. The house was a labyrinth inside, far larger than it had appeared from the exterior.

There had to be a thousand cats. Each one different, but none distinct.

Mayhem appeared in the middle of the room, looking around with interest. She fluttered out of reach, sniffing the air, but didn't seem interested in any particular cat.

"If this is supposed to be a challenge, maybe it's the biggest cat?" I asked.

"Like a lion?"

I shrugged. "There's every other breed in here."

"Every other breed of house cat."

"Fine." But he was right. This was some kind of trick. Or test. I'd used my lightning and water magic during the race. Maybe this required one of my gifts.

I had healing, illusion, and acute senses. Since I couldn't figure out how healing and illusion would help me, I perked my ears and tried to hear something unique.

Heimdall's magic flowed through me as my hearing focused. Suddenly, I could pick up a thousand different heartbeats. Light and fast. Then two others—slower, louder. Me and Cade.

And a third.

"Holy crap," I whispered. "There's another heartbeat here. It's different than ours and the cats'."

"Could that be the one you're looking for?"

"Maybe." I followed my hearing, moving slowly through the rooms and passing by hundreds of cats. Some of them looked curious, some looked pissed, and most just slept.

Mayhem followed along, staying out of reach of the cats' claws.

The heartbeat that I sought grew louder and louder as I

neared. Finally, we reached a sitting room that looked no different than the rest. Lots of furniture, lots of cats.

And one cat, sleeping in the middle of the room, which had a heartbeat as loud as a drum.

I pointed to him. "That's him, but he's not any different than the rest."

"Even I can hear his heartbeat," Cade said. "Just barely, but it's louder than the rest."

The cat was gray and small, stretched out on a little bed that was shaped like a heart. Mayhem fluttered over to the cat, looking at it with suspicion. It was the first one she'd shown interest in, which only went to prove my theory.

I approached slowly. "This is weird. It's too easy."

Would he turn into a tiger when I touched him? What the heck was this?

"How can I help?" Cade said. "Normally I'd have an idea of what's needed but this...this is strange."

"No kidding." I stopped a few feet from the cat and stretched out my hand, gently touching his back. His fur was soft, and he stretched, his little toes pointing outward.

Then he started purring.

"What the crap?" I shifted closer, petting him again.

He stretched and purred louder.

This was going too well.

Tension thrummed through my muscles as I got closer, stopping when I stood over the cat. I scooped one hand under his side and wrapped my other around his middle, pulling him upright. I got him up on his feet and tried to pick him up, but he stopped solid.

He kept purring.

I pulled, but it was like he was nailed to the heart bed. Except the cat didn't seem to mind a bit. As hard as I pulled, he stayed right where he was, standing like he was waiting for his food bowl to be filled.

"What's wrong?" Cade asked.

"I can't pick him up." I panted, pulling on the cat's middle like I was trying to heave a thousand-pound block off the floor.

Mayhem fluttered by my head, confused and wary.

"What the hell kind of magic is this?" I demanded.

"Want me to try?"

"Sure." We were technically allowed to complete the challenge together, after all.

Cade bent over the cat, wrapping his big hands around the creature's middle. He tried picking him up, but jerked to a stop.

"Aye, that's weird." He pulled harder, face turning red.

The cat didn't move. His fur didn't even rustle, and he never stopped purring.

Finally, Cade stepped back, sweat dripping down his brow. "He's not moving an inch."

"Let me try again." I moved toward the cat, wrapping my hands around his waist and pulling.

Nothing.

I pulled harder, mind racing. There was something weird about this cat. I could hear its insanely loud heartbeat. And its fur felt weird under my hands all of a sudden.

Almost scaly. But smooth. And rough.

What was going on?

A sense that something was *wrong* filled me.

Not true.

The words filtered through my mind.

Not true.

I shook my head, but the words continued to echo. It was vaguely similar to what happened when a new power came online. But this one was telling me that something was false about this situation.

I strained, trying to pick up the cat, as visions flashed in my mind. They clouded my head, fuzzing my thoughts.

A giant serpent appeared in my mind—thousands of miles long and hundreds wide. Fear raced through me, freezing in my veins as I struggled with the cat.

On the outside, the situation was ridiculous. I was struggling to pick up a ten-pound cat.

But in my mind, I was underneath a massive serpent, fighting a battle to keep it from crushing me. It was a creature so large that my mind couldn't conceive of it. Green scales covered the beast—like the ones I *swore* I could feel on the cat.

Its weight pressed me down. My chest tightened, breath rushing from my lungs. Panic filled me like acid. I pushed at the serpent, whose belly was crushing me into the dirt. I had become trapped under the beast somehow, and its great weight would kill me.

I gasped, straining, giving it everything I had. Blackness clouded the edges of my vision.

Not true.

The voice echoed again, fainter this time.

I shook my head, my brain and my body in two separate places. One fought the weight of the serpent, the other tried to pick up the cat.

I had to do something different. It was nearly impossible to breathe now, my mind convincing me that the scene playing out in my head was real.

But it couldn't be, could it?

I gasped, yanking my hands away from the cat's belly.

Pick up the cat.

Utgard-Loki's words echoed in my head. I had to pick up this damn cat. Somehow.

I reached for its front paw, wrapping my hands around the little leg. The tiny creature kept purring—I'd have felt ridiculous if my mind weren't convinced I was fighting a giant serpent's weight.

I yanked as hard as I could, pulling the leg with everything I had.

Finally, the weight on my chest decreased. The serpent that was crushing me in my mind lifted. The paw rose off the ground. Just an inch.

But it was enough for me to roll out from underneath the body of the serpent.

In the real world—the one not inside my own crazy mind—I let go of the cat's paw and flung myself away from it, landing on the rug.

Panting, I stared at the ceiling. I rubbed my chest, still feeling the ache of the serpent's weight.

"Are you all right?" Cade appeared above me, leaning down, a look of concern on his face.

"Yeah." I struggled to catch my breath. "I have no idea what just happened. It was like I was trying not to be crushed by a giant snake."

"All I saw was a slightly annoyed cat."

I scowled at him.

"Not that you're wrong." He held up his hands, placating.

I rubbed my head. "I think it was all in my mind, but I can't quite figure it out."

"What are you doing here!?" The screech made Cade fly backward and me jump up.

I was on my feet a half second later, heart thundering. Cade had turned to face an old woman. She was skinny and small, with a lined face and gray hair. Her dark clothes looked like a strange, ragged cloak.

"I'm sorry. We were told to come here."

"And pester my cats?!" She was so irate that I thought her head might turn purple.

We'd met the ultimate cat lady. Not that I liked to play off stereotypes. But she was a lady and she had a *lot* of cats.

"I'm sorry. Utgard-Loki told me to come here." And he'd also told me to fight someone.

When the old lady flew at me, fast as a rocket, my brain stutter-stepped. He couldn't possibly mean *her?*

The confusion cost me.

She delivered a jump-kick to my chest that sent me crashing into the wall. Pain flared in my whole body, and through cloudy eyes, I caught sight of her whirl like a tornado and hit Cade with another kick. He flew into the opposite wall, scattering cats that hissed and yowled with rage.

The little gray cat had lain back down on the heart bed in the middle of the floor, completely unconcerned, as the rest of the cats fled.

Yep, something was weird about that cat.

I scrambled to my feet and approached the old woman, my hands raised. "I don't want to fight."

"Well, *I* do." She cackled and raced for me, raising her fist.

I dodged, and she hit the air. Then she came at me with her other hand, landing a blow to my cheek that sent me spinning like a top.

She shrieked her glee and jumped on me. I thrashed as she wrapped her arms around me, squeezing my middle so tight that a rib cracked.

I could freaking *hear* it.

The pain nearly made me vomit.

Her hold broke suddenly, and I spun to see Cade yank her off me. He hesitated, a mistake I'd never seen him make, and she used it to her advantage, turning and swinging for him with her mean right hook.

Like me, he was fast enough to dodge the first, but not the

second. She nailed him in the cheek, having to strike upward in an awkward position since he was so tall.

The power was there, however, because Cade spun around, blood flying from his mouth.

Holy fates, this was no normal old woman.

Truth.

Okay, weird. I had a new power that didn't know when to assert itself. I didn't need it to tell me this old lady wasn't normal, that was for sure.

She lunged for Cade, her arms outstretched in a maneuver I knew would allow her to break his ribs. I lunged for her, grabbing her around the waist and swinging her away from him. I let go, sending her flying across the room.

Fast as a snake, she got her balance and turned on me, lunging and throwing me to the ground. She went down with me, straddling my waist. Her grip dug into my shoulders, crushing.

Pain flared and tears burned my eyes. I punched, nailing her in the cheek. She barely twitched.

For a second, a vision flashed in my mind, making it look like a black cloak covered her. Pain flared again, driving the image from my head.

I pushed her shoulders, trying to heave her off of me.

She didn't budge. Now that I wasn't catching her by surprise, she couldn't be moved. She was just too damned strong. She couldn't weigh more than a hundred pounds, but she stayed stuck to me, her hands moving toward my throat to strangle me.

Crap!

I needed to be stronger.

I pushed, giving it everything I had. Suddenly, strength flowed through my muscles. Energy and power.

Use it.

The voice echoed in my head.

Use it.

Oh fates! This was another new gift. I pushed harder, and she budged a few inches. Cade appeared behind her, grabbing her shoulders and pulling hard.

But she was ready for him this time—or ready for me, maybe. Either way, she didn't move.

So I pushed harder, using the new magic that flowed through me. It was physical strength—like a freaking Olympian's. I shoved, finally heaving her off me, then leapt onto her.

We wrestled, rolling over each other on the ground as we tried to land our hits. She seemed to deliver more, though maybe it seemed that way because every one hurt like the devil. My whole body felt bruised as we fought our way across the floor.

Any guilt I'd had over beating up an old person was long gone.

No matter how hard we fought, neither of us could get the upper hand. And Cade couldn't get a move in edgewise. She'd move out of his way like a snake, or lash out with a quick fist.

Even Mayhem tried, but the woman dodged her flame easily.

I didn't know how long we fought, but eventually, we both lay side by side, panting. Every inch of me ached like it'd been run over by a train. Like a billion trains had run over me, each one squishing a single cell.

Through bleary eyes, I saw Cade on the other side of the room, collapsed like us. Somehow, she'd managed to beat him up, too, laying out both of us like we were rookies in a major league fighting ring. Or whatever it was called, where super fighters fought. My brain was mush and no longer working.

Noise sounded from beside me, and I looked over. The old woman heaved herself to her feet and turned to me.

I stared death in the eyes.

She would kill me. There was no way I could win this. Every bone felt broken. Every muscle torn.

"Enough!" The voice boomed down from above.

Utgard-Loki.

Please be calling it quits.

The old woman glared at me, then turned and left.

I groaned, gratitude welling up inside me.

"You okay?" I asked Cade.

He groaned. "Just had my arse kicked by an old woman."

I laughed. A cat appeared, looking down at me. Then it bit my nose.

"Hey!" I tried to swat at it, but my arm was too injured to move.

I lay still, calling upon my healing power as the cat stared down at me, green eyes flashing. It was a calico, and really pretty despite the annoyance in its eyes. Something poked under my back, soft and squishy.

Once my muscles and bones had mended—bringing with it sweet relief—I rolled over, praying I wasn't crushing a cat.

I looked behind me, spotting a crumpled blue fluffy thing.

A cat bed.

Whew.

The calico curled up in the bed, glaring at me.

"Sorry. Sorry." I struggled to my feet, finally able to move.

Cade limped to me. "Let's get out of here."

"Amen." I leaned against him, and we stumbled through the house. Mayhem disappeared. "I sure hope we won."

"It's not looking great."

"I don't know." Memories flashed in my mind. "It wasn't as simple as it appeared."

"That old lady certainly wasn't simple."

"They never are." I limped out the front door and looked up at Utgard-Loki.

He scowled down at me.

Before I could say anything, a hand picked me up by the back of my jacket. I swung limply. "I'm getting sick of this shit!"

Utgard-Loki laughed. If I'd been big enough to punch him, I'd have given him the Old Lady Special.

I healed the rest of my injuries as they carried us back to the main hall. The place was just as huge as ever, and with my depleted strength and magic, it was even scarier. Especially since we failed the contests.

Or had we?

Something kept bugging me about what had happened. Actually, many somethings. The cat's scaly body, the visions of the serpent, the way the old woman's image had flickered to reveal someone wearing a cloak. Someone like death. The man who raced us.

Hugi.

The name...

So familiar.

I'd read it somewhere. And it was similar to Huginn's name. Huginn, the raven whose name meant *thought*.

That was it! Hugi was *thought*. No one could be as fast as a thought.

Annoyance streaked through me.

We'd been had.

My captor set me on the table. I couldn't help but notice it had been set with enormous silver plates.

Because we were to be dinner? We'd hardly be a snack. We were what got stuck in a giant's teeth.

"Well?" I shouted up. "Did we win?"

Cade chuckled.

I glanced at him and whispered, "Can you tell I'm fed up?"

"Just a little." He grinned, but the smile faded. "Though we might be about to become giant chow."

I looked up at Utgard-Loki. Syn had come to stand beside him. She was in her larger giant form, though as a god, she should be roughly my size.

Had she given me her magic back in the cottage so I could see that something wasn't truthful about the cat?

She inclined her head to me.

She had!

"You did not win," Utgard-Loki said. "And now you will become dinner."

"Not true!" I shouted it. I *felt* it. He was lying. Syn's power raced through me. I could *feel* that he was lying. "The contest was rigged."

"Oh, how so?"

"Hugi! You tried to make us race *thought*. No one can outrun their thoughts."

Utgard-Loki grumbled.

"And something was weird about that cat." That was when Syn's powers had come into play. "It was a giant snake. Jörmungandr?"

I guessed the name of the world snake, the serpent that was wrapped around the earth. I just threw the name out there, having no idea if it was true, but it was the only snake I could think of besides Níðhöggr, and that snake had looked different than the one in my vision.

Utgard-Loki grumbled, but Syn said, "Truth."

"Thank you!" I glared at Utgard-Loki. "You're the trickster Jötunn, and you're trying to pull a trick on us. What was the deal with that damned snake?"

"Magic, of course," he said. "The cat was actually Jörmungandr, as you guessed. And you lifted him up. Just a little."

I wanted to fist pump my victory. "When I lifted his paw?"

"Yes. How did you do it?"

"I am the Valkyrie Dragon God. Of course I could do it." Because a god had given me power. A god of strength. Had to be Magni, son of Thor. I looked at Syn, who seemed to understand me. "Magni?"

She nodded.

"Did you give me the power of discerning the truth?" I asked.

"I did, but you are weak with it. Unable to interpret. That will take practice."

"You what?" Utgard-Loki bellowed.

She smacked him on the arm, a dismissive gesture more than a violent one. "I am a guest, Utgard-Loki, and I do as I see fit. The gods support Bree—most of us, at least. We assisted her with that challenge—though some of us made it more difficult for her as well."

I remembered the water pressing in on me. And the lightning striking. "The water and lightning?"

She nodded. "You need to prove that you're worthy of your gifts. By now, word has gotten out about your request for the rest of your powers. Some of the gods are testing you, seeing if you are the master of your magic."

I guessed that was fair, but I didn't like it.

At least I'd passed. Or felt like I'd passed, anyway.

I turned my face up toward Utgard-Loki. "Who was the old woman? Death?"

"Old age. It gets everyone in the end."

"She hasn't gotten me yet."

"No, she hasn't."

"So, I'm not dinner, then. I did well enough that I didn't lose."

"You could still be dinner," he grumbled.

"We made a deal," I insisted. "You have to live up to it."

"The other gods and immortals would not look kindly on you betraying your word," Cade said. "I know how important your honor is to you."

He sounded so damned reasonable. Persuasive.

Utgard-Loki seemed mollified. "Fine. You didn't *win*, but you didn't lose. So you can ask Syn one question. Not three."

She looked at him with an arched brow. "You tell me what to do?"

He sighed. "I ask."

She nodded imperiously. "Good." She looked down at us. "We will meet in my quarters."

"Thank you."

She picked me up by the back of my jacket and I scowled. This sucked.

But since I was hoping to sweet-talk some more answers out of her, I kept my mouth shut as she carried Cade and me from the room. I waved to Utgard-Loki as we passed through the huge doors.

Syn set us down. Magic swirled around her, and she shrank down until she was our size.

"This way." She gestured for us to follow, and we did.

A few minutes later, we stopped in a beautifully decorated room that had probably been a broom closet for the giants but made a massive suite for a human-sized person. Windows had been carved out of the wall, but because the stone wall was so thick—properly done, for a giant's castle—there appeared to be a tunnel between the glass and the actual room.

"You seek Idun?" Syn turned, her glittering blue dress matching the blue decor in the room. The whole space was done in blue silks and pale white wood, suiting her.

"We do. Odin and Frigg are growing old. The other gods must be, too."

She touched her face, and I realized that she'd expertly

applied makeup to cover the wrinkles and age spots. I hated that she was suffering, but that meant she had something at stake here, too.

"I need to find her so that the gods will grant me the rest of my powers. Without them, I'll never defeat the Rebel Gods."

"Evildoers," she scolded.

I wanted to ask what she knew about them, but didn't want to waste my question.

"I am not a seer," she said. "So I cannot see into the future. There may not be much I can do for you. But I can tell you if something is true or false. So don't waste your question."

"Okay." I looked at Cade. "Any ideas?"

He shook his head.

The thing that we most wanted to know was whether or not she was here like Mímir said—and that was all that Syn could truly answer. "Is Idun here now or has she been in the past?"

"She is not, and never has been."

"Damn. Why did Mímir send us here, then?"

Her eyes sharpened. "Mímir?"

"Yes. Do you know him?"

"Know him, but don't trust him."

Exactly what the fox and the eagle had said. Don't trust the wise man. But we *had* trusted him, and he'd sent us here. To a place where we'd nearly died and Idun had never been. Why would he have done that?

A thought tugged at my mind.

"What is Mímir?" I asked. "He's not god of wisdom, is he?"

"He is not. He is a Jötunn."

"But he doesn't live in Jötunheimr."

"They do not want him here. He's of the smaller variety, so this place isn't built for him. And he has never been fond of his own kind."

Oh, fates. I looked at Cade. Interest gleamed in his eyes. And suspicion.

"Mímir sent us here to die." An idea flared to life. "Which he would do because *he* stole Idun. He can't fight us with his current body, so he had to get rid of us."

Syn's sharp gaze met my own. "A body? Really?"

"He's built himself a body using magic." My mind whirled.

"The apples are giving his new body strength," Cade said. "Like the fox said. The apples aren't only for immortality. They're for strength as well. They're keeping his borrowed body alive."

A memory tugged. "The splash in the well. Maybe that's where Idun is. Maybe that's why Odin can't see her from his throne."

"It seems that you don't need me," Syn said. "Because that sounds very likely."

I turned to her. "Wait. I do need you, though. This power you gave me... How do I use it?"

"It's not like other gods' powers. Not as straightforward as creating lightning or using your strength. It will allow you to interpret the truthfulness of someone's statement. And in times of great need, it may allow you to see that illusions are not true."

"Like Jörmungandr the house cat?"

"Exactly." She smiled. "The more you use it, the stronger it may become. Maybe. I don't know. I've never given my power to anyone before."

"Thank you for giving it to me."

"I believe in you, Bree Blackwood. I think that you will become the master of your magic. And with it, you will defeat the Rebel Gods."

Oh fates, I hoped she was right. Because I had a long way to go before either of those things happened.

12

Fortunately, Syn gave us a ride back to the portal that would escort us from Jötunheimr back to Mímir's well. It was vastly superior to ride on her shoulders. If I was never carried by the scruff of my neck again, it would be too soon.

The view from up there was fabulous, too. In the distance, I could see Hraesvelgr, the giant eagle, soaring high in the air. Every time he flapped his wings, a breeze rustled my hair. I also spotted the giant fox, asleep where he had been earlier.

"This way, they can't pester me for their apples," I said.

"Aye, this is the way to travel." Cade looked up at Syn's face. "Thank you for the ride!"

"I don't mind." She strode through the forest, her size more at scale with the huge trees.

When she dropped us off, she leaned down. "Remember—Mímir is tricky. He has to be, to survive. So keep your wits about you."

"Thank you," I said.

"No—thank you. We need Idun and her apples." She touched her cheek, and like before, I could see the makeup if I looked closely. "I'm glad that you were clever enough to determine who abducted her."

"Mímir was clever, trying to drive us away. I wouldn't be surprised if he was the one who planted the story that a Jötunn abducted her."

"Likely, he did. He doesn't look like one, after all. No one would suspect him."

"Well, I do." I grinned. "And now we're going to go rescue Idun."

"Safe travels." She turned and left.

I pressed my fingertips to the comms charm at my throat, and the magic ignited. "Ana? Rowan?"

"Bree!" Ana's voice echoed through. "We found the crystals!"

"Oh, excellent."

"Have you got all your power yet?"

"No, but hopefully soon."

"We'll be ready when you do. Hedy is preparing the spell that will help us feed our magic into the crystals, then we should be ready to set up the ambush."

"Perfect." All I had to do was rescue Idun. "I'll be back soon, I hope. Just wish me luck."

"Good luck. We're all rooting for you."

"Thanks." I grinned, and removed my fingertips. The magic faded. I held out my hand to Cade. "Ready to go get Idun?"

"Absolutely."

We stepped onto the wide, flat root that was the strange portal leading down to Mímir's well. The ether sucked us in immediately, sending us on a whirlwind ride down the side of the tree. The wind whipped at my hair, and my stomach leapt into my throat.

By the time we reached the bottom, my head was spinning. I clutched at Cade, catching my breath. He was looking a bit green about the gills as well.

"The magic here is intense," he said.

"Understatement." I stepped off the root, surveying our surroundings.

The massive boulders loomed on all sides, tumbling around the base of Yggdrasil and providing many places to hide. Shadows stretched long against the ground, though I had no idea where they were coming from, since I couldn't see a sun. I wasn't even sure if there *was* a sun around Yggdrasil.

Cade joined me, his head cocked as he listened. "Where do you think he'll be?"

"No idea." I engaged Heimdall's power of hearing, creeping toward a boulder and trying to stay in the shadows. "He may have been alerted to our arrival. That portal may give off some magic when it's in operation."

Cade joined me, crouched low against the stone. He was in hunter mode, and I could almost see the wolf through his skin.

I tried to envision where the well had been. About fifty yards from here, hidden amongst the boulders, if I was remembering properly.

Something flashed out of the corner of my eye. A green potion bomb exploded against the boulder at my side.

I ducked as Cade drew his shield from the ether, concealing us. I'd been too slow. The green liquid had flecked my face and neck. It burned like acid—hell, it probably *was* acid—and I winced, wiping it away.

"To the right!" Cade said.

I turned to look, peering over the edge of his shield and searching the shadows in the direction that the potion bomb had flown from. Mímir didn't have a lot of magic, so the potion bombs made sense.

My hearing picked up the faintest trace of his heartbeat—irregular and inhuman. Who knew what kind of heart he had in his pieced-together body?

I drew my own shield and crept forward hurriedly, following the beat of the heart. It moved away from us, and I quickened my pace, adrenaline racing through my veins. Cat and mouse—except the mouse was armed with some mean-ass potion bombs.

When a rope tugged at my ankle, my mind blanked in shock.

It jerked me upward, tugging me upside down until I dangled ten feet above the ground. A scream strangled in my throat, but I bit it back—no need to let Mímir know that his trap had worked.

"Hang on!" Cade whispered.

Blood rushed to my head as I hung upside down with my heart thundering in my ears. The rope cut into my ankle. I kept my shield up, frantically trying to figure out where Mímir was.

Cade scaled a huge boulder, then drew his sword and leapt. He flew through the air gracefully and sliced his blade through the rope that kept me aloft.

I flailed in midair, managing to land on my hands and knees instead of my head.

Cade landed next to me.

"Good work," I whispered, scrambling to my feet and brushing the dirt off my hands.

Something exploded against my back and panic flared. Fast as I could, I stripped my jacket off. Cade helped, yanking it from my hands and flinging the acid-covered leather away from us. My back burned like hell where it had soaked through, but the damage was minimal.

We darted away, shields raised, and found cover in a crevice between two rocks. We crouched low, raising our shields to protect us from his acid bombs.

Mímir's heartbeat sounded in the distance. Maybe ten yards away. Twenty? It was hard to say without knowing how loud it should actually be. Since it wasn't human, I couldn't tell.

A splash sounded.

"Hear that?" I whispered.

"Aye. Just like before."

"She's in the well. And he's trying to distract us." I peered over my shield, but could only make out boulders and a huge tree root twisting around them. "Can you distract him while I search for Idun?"

"Aye."

I kissed him, my heart thundering with a strange combo of fight anxiety and attraction. I liked Cade in fight mode—but that was not what I should be focusing on right now. I darted away, keeping my footsteps silent.

Behind me, Cade shouted, "Hey, Mímir! Is that the best you've got?"

I sprinted silently, listening for Mímir's heartbeat or footsteps. They sounded softly in the distance. He was running toward Cade.

Worry crept into my mind, but I shoved it away. I'd always worry for Cade—hard not to, when I loved him—but he could handle this.

And I had a job to do.

I reached the stone well, which was larger than I remembered. Twenty feet across, at least. Wide enough for me to fly out of, thank fates. But the descent would be trickier. I hadn't mastered that.

I leaned over the edge and caught sight of stone blocks protruding from the walls. Bingo. They'd make great handholds.

Quick as I could, I stowed my shield in the ether, scrambled onto the well wall, and climbed in, grabbing onto the stone handholds that had seen a lot of action over the years. This had to be how Mímir got in, too.

I scrambled down the wall, deeper into the cool dark. It smelled of water and moss. Magic swirled on the air as I climbed down. Strange, since Mímir didn't have much to speak of.

But his wisdom came from this well, didn't it?

A splash sounded below.

Idun?

I looked down, just in time to see an enormous sea serpent shoot out of the water, headed straight for me. Its fangs glinted in the light, and its breath reeked of dead bodies.

Oh shit!

My heart jumped.

All I had was a puny dagger. I didn't bother drawing it. Didn't have time, anyway. I just pressed myself against the stone and squeezed my eyes closed.

The beast's head slammed into me, but his fangs didn't puncture. The blow crushed me against the stone wall, and I tightened my grip, trying desperately not to fall off.

One of the monster's fangs caught in the waistband of my pants, scraping against my skin. As gravity dragged the creature backward, it pulled me with it. I lost my grip on the wall and plummeted, still attached to the serpent.

We crashed into the water. It closed over my head, cold and sharp. Panic tightened in my chest. I flailed and kicked, beating at the serpent until its fang released my waistband. I kicked away, smacking the creature in the face, and pushed up through the water.

My head broke the surface, and I gasped, my heart thundering a wild cadence.

Holy fates.

I kicked, my head spinning from the fall and the lack of oxygen.

The creature was *under* me. I could feel it in the water, my magic sensing how it slithered down below. It was about to strike, to burst upward and devour me in one bite.

Icy fear pierced me.

Think.

I looked around, frantic, and caught sight of an open door located partway up the well's shaft. I must have missed it as I was plummeting with the serpent.

Quickly, I called on my magic, forcing the water to carry me upward. I tried to use it to push the serpent down, but I had no idea if it worked. The water rose quickly, forcing me toward the entrance to the well.

Right as I passed the doorway, I grabbed it and scrambled in. A loud hiss sounded from behind me, and I looked back, spotting the serpent's bright eyes staring right at me.

Down!

I commanded the water to rush downward. It did, dragging the serpent along with it. The beast's fangs caught on the edge of the stone wall, scraping against the rock as it tried to cling on. I scrambled over and kicked it in the nose, shoving it off the ledge.

Then I fell backward, panting.

Holy fates.

I struggled to catch my breath. That had been a wild ride. Shaking, I climbed to my feet.

The passage was short and unlit, but the room beyond glowed with golden light. I drew my dagger and shield for good measure, and crept quietly down the hall. Shouts echoed from above. Cade must be harassing Mímir, trying to distract him.

Keep it up.

The magic smelled dark down here, evil in a way that I hadn't smelled from up above.

As soon as I stepped into the main room of Mímir's house, smoke flashed. It exploded from all angles, clogging my lungs and blinding me. Coughing, I staggered backward.

Right into the grip of a huge person. Massive arms wrapped around me, and my heart jumped into my throat. The arms were covered with scales, the fingers tipped with claws. They dug into my side, pain flaring as blood welled.

Shit!

I dropped my weight heavily, surprising the creature so that it loosened its grip. It growled, a low sound that sent fear streaking through me.

"Go for the stomach!" a feminine voice cried.

I spun and struck out with my dagger, following the advice and plunging my blade into the monster's middle. My attacker wore armor, but it was damaged right in the stomach. I diverted my blade a half-inch, and stabbed right through the hole in the armor, sinking into skin.

The creature roared, and I looked up, catching sight of burning red eyes and long black horns.

Demon.

Here to guard Idun.

I yanked my blade free, shoving the demon in the chest. He stumbled backward, clutching his stomach. I shoved him again, determined to get him into the well. That would keep the serpent distracted.

We were only halfway down the hall when he rallied, yanking his arms away and drawing a huge sword from the sheath at his side. He swung out, and I raised my shield. The blade clanged against it, sending vibrations up my arm.

I grunted. "You're going to have to do better than that."

He growled again, the scent of rotten fish washing over me.

"Your magic is rank." I kicked him in the stomach, and he hissed in pain, stumbling backward. I kicked again, aiming for the same place.

Without my sword, it was my best bet.

Finally, he stumbled off the back ledge, not realizing that he'd already reached it. His shocked eyes met mine as he tumbled into the darkness.

A splash sounded below.

I didn't hang around to watch. So not my style.

Instead, I spun and raced back into the house. The smoke had dissipated some, but it was still hard to see.

"Idun!" I called.

"Back here!"

I hurried through the cluttered room, dodging furniture and other bits and bobs. The decor was ornate for such a weird place, but all of it looked to be old and in disrepair. Near the back, chained to a wall, I found a beautiful blonde woman. Her white dress was dirty and her hair knotted. A basket of shining red apples sat next to her.

"Idun!" I fell to my knees at her side, inspecting the chain around her ankle. "Is there anyone else here?"

"Not if you killed the guard and Mímir. Who are you?"

"Bree Blackwood." I picked up the heavy chain. "Valkyrie Dragon God."

"Oh." Interest sounded in her voice. "Isn't this my lucky day?"

"I hope so." I gripped the chain in both hands and yanked, praying my new strength would do the job.

The chain rattled and clanked, straining, but didn't break.

"Shit."

"You really think you can break that?"

"I have Magni's strength."

"Oh. Well, try again, then!"

I didn't have a shot at breaking the metal, but it was sunk into the stone wall. That had potential.

"Move over," I said.

She shifted left, and I braced my feet against the wall, gripping the chain and yanking with all my might. Magic flowed through my muscles, giving them an unnatural, godly strength.

The chain strained, and the stone seemed to creak. Finally, the stone cracked, the chain's anchor pulling out.

I flew backward, slamming my head onto the ground.

Pain flared as my vision doubled.

Fates, I need to practice.

"Well done!" Idun said.

Aching, I scrambled up. "Thanks."

She grabbed her basket of apples and handed one to me. "Here. This will give you strength."

"It won't make me live extra long, right?" I wanted a nice, normal-length life, ideally departing the world at the same time as my sisters and Cade. I didn't want to hang around after they were gone, twiddling my thumbs and lonely.

"No. Just greater strength and better health for the next few days."

I could definitely use some of that. I took the apple she handed me and bit in, chomping down as I bent to pick up her chain. I chewed and spoke at the same time. "Let's get out of here."

I carried the chain that dangled from her ankle, polishing off the sweet fruit as we hurried down the tunnel. At the exit into the well's shaft, I stopped and peered down. All was quiet and calm.

Which meant that the serpent had eaten the demon and was waiting once again.

"I don't know if I can climb that," Idun said. "I tried before and failed."

"That's okay." The apple really had made me feel strong. Combined with Magni's strength, I could probably fly us out of here. "I think I can carry you."

"Really?" She gave me a skeptical look.

I flared my wings out, and her brows rose. "I'm willing to try."

"Then so am I."

"Great. Hold on to your apples." I held out my arms and picked her up, damsel-in-distress style. "I feel like a knight in shining armor."

"What is that?"

Right. They'd come about five hundred years after the Vikings. "I'll explain later."

I walked to the very edge of the tunnel. Idun felt light in my arms, which was really freaking strange. I sucked in a deep breath and jumped off the ledge, flaring my wings wide.

We fell for half a second, then my moving wings caught the air, and I hurtled upward. Below, a splash sounded. I looked down.

The serpent shot out of the water, headed straight for us.

Shit!

I gave it my all, flying as hard as I could, and shot from the well, high into the sky. The serpent breached the mouth of the well, its fangs snapping the air right below us. Idun's arms tightened around my neck.

Then the serpent fell, missing its target. I laughed and shot higher, searching the ground for Cade. He and Mímir were having a standoff. Mímir on one boulder, Cade on another. Mímir hurled potion bombs at Cade, who dodged them. Mostly.

What should we do with Mímir?

It wasn't my place to kill him, even though he was evil. We didn't have time, anyway.

"We're not going to take out Mímir," I said. "Let's just get out of here."

"Agreed." Idun's voice was eager.

"Cade!" I shouted. "Let's get out of here."

He looked up and grinned. A swirl of golden light flashed around him, and he shifted. The giant wolf leapt off the boulder and raced for the portal that led out of Mímir's realm.

I flew over his head, following Cade. The wise man looked up, his crazed eyes meeting mine.

"Thief!" he screamed, spit flying from his lips. I'd never seen anyone so enraged.

"Kidnapping psychopath!" I yelled.

For good measure, I sent a bolt of lightning at him. He dodged, but it kept him busy.

As quickly as I could, I flew after Cade, Idun in my arms. It was surprisingly easy to carry her now that I had Magni's strength and had eaten the apple.

When we were far enough away that Mímir was no longer pursuing us, I landed next to Cade, who shifted back to human. Carefully, I set Idun on the ground.

"Thank you," she said.

"Do you know how to get us back to Asgard?" I asked.

"Yes. There's a portal just a couple miles away from here."

"You can ride on my back," Cade said.

She eyed him appreciatively, and I kind of wanted to step on her foot. But I was bigger than that. And it was a good idea.

Cade shifted back to his wolf form, and Idun climbed on. I took to the air, and we hurried toward the portal, Idun directing the way. It didn't take long to reach it, and as we stepped in, I was certain I heard Mímir's angry cursing following us back to Asgard.

13

By the time we arrived in Asgard, I was ready to get the hell out of there and get a shower. The stink of the well water clung to me, and I felt like I was covered by a thin layer of slime.

Idun had a definite pep in her step, however.

"Thank you so much for rescuing me," she said as we climbed the stairs to Odin's palace. "I was so stupid, walking · alone near Mímir's well. He hasn't lived there for years."

"He escaped Odin, though I don't know how."

Idun frowned and shook her head. "I always thought it was a bad idea, keeping his head like that."

"Will he survive without your apples?"

"I don't know. His head probably will, because Odin enchanted it. As for the rest of him..."

"It's Odin's problem," Cade said.

I liked the sound of that, because I didn't want to see creepy birdgoatman again if I could help it.

Before we stepped through the great doors, I turned to Idun. "I wouldn't have been able to rescue you without the help from Hraesvelgr the eagle or the ice fox in Jötunheimr. They requested an apple, though. Will you give them one?"

She smiled and nodded. "I know the fox and the eagle. I'll see it done."

"Good." I smiled, relieved. "Because I really don't want either one coming after me for failing to fulfill my end of the bargain."

"No, you certainly do not." She stepped through the great door, and I followed.

Odin and Frigg were waiting for us when we were shown into their throne room. They both rose off their throne as we entered, grins splitting their faces.

"Well done, Valkyrie!" Odin boomed.

"Idun!" Frigg swept off the dais. "Are you well?"

"I am, thanks to Bree."

Frigg turned appraising eyes to me. "You truly are worthy of your magic."

Odin strode toward us, inspecting me. "You did well. I witnessed your heroics from my throne. Some of the gods even gave you challenges, and you passed." He looked at Idun. "As for you, it was wise for Mímir to hide you in his well. You were hidden by knowledge I did not have. I sought him there a few months ago, but found neither hide nor hair of him."

"He's stronger than we thought," Idun said.

Odin tsked and shook his head. "My mistake."

"It was." Frigg gave him a stern look, then turned to me. "As for you—the gods will grant you what you request. And I will be able to give you a shielding charm that will protect you for twenty-four hours. I'm afraid it's the longest that any charm can hold up against the powerful magic flowing through you."

"Thank you." Twenty-four hours would be hugely helpful.

"Wait here." She drifted away.

Odin reached out, touching Idun's chain, which I still gripped in my hands like a weird leash. It disintegrated, and she grinned, handing him an apple.

Odin just grunted and turned, walking back to his throne and chomping on the fruit.

A man of few words.

Idun turned to Cade and me. "Thank you again."

"Of course," I said.

She left the room, her basket of apples clutched in her hand. She passed Frigg on the way, handing her an apple. The goddess took a bite, seeming to glow with health as soon as she swallowed. By the time she reached us, she looked vastly younger. Twenty-five, at most.

Frigg handed me a little vial of potion. "Drink."

I did as she commanded, swallowing the sweet liquid. Magic shivered over me, and I felt insubstantial for just a moment.

"Now the Rebel Gods can't find me?"

"For twenty-four hours," she said. "Ready for the rest of your magic?"

"I am." That wasn't the whole truth, but I didn't have a lot of choice in the matter. This was happening no matter what.

"Odin!" Frigg called. "Make the circle."

Odin got off his throne and ambled toward the center of the room. He drew a golden sword from the ether and pressed the tip to the stone floor. Light glowed brightly, shooting out from the sword and creating a circle. Magic pricked on the air, dozens of different signatures.

"He's calling the gods," Frigg said.

"They'll come here?" Cade asked.

"Not physically, no. But they'll be here." She gestured for me to enter the circle.

I did, the magic sparkling over my skin as I stepped into the middle. It felt like being submerged in a bath of champagne.

Odin and Frigg met my gaze.

"It will take everything you have to succeed against the Rebel Gods," Frigg said.

"And succeed, you must." Odin's voice was heavy with seriousness.

"But you are the champion of the Vikings," Frigg said. "You have proved that here today. You are capable, Bree. And we believe in you."

It was the last thing I heard before the lightning struck me. Pain shot through me, followed by the electric pulse of magic. So many signatures, so much power. I could hardly bear it.

I staggered, going to my knees.

All around, shadows appeared. They were human shaped, but indistinct. The gods?

One by one, powers flowed into me. Magic that I didn't recognize, but would hopefully learn. I tried to stay conscious, but the pain was too much. Overwhelming.

Cade's shout was the last thing I heard.

I woke up in Cade's arms. The air was chilly and smelled of Scotland. He was carrying me across the Protectorate lawn, but he was the only thing I could see.

"Hey." The words were scratchy in my throat.

He looked down, so handsome it was hard to believe. "Hey."

"I love you."

His brows rose, a look of surprised happiness on his face. "You do?"

"Of course." I felt it like the warmth of the sun, radiating out from me. Or maybe radiating out from him. Whatever it was, it was warm and wonderful. And it was definitely love.

"You're hardly conscious. Are you sure you want to stick by that?" he asked.

"I've known for a while. And I wanted to tell you when it was the right time. Not when I was just repeating your words back to you."

"That's now?"

"Definitely." Maybe the timing was kind of weird, but I couldn't hold it in any longer.

I leaned up and pressed a kiss to his lips, falling into the joy of him. I didn't add that now was the time because I wasn't sure if I would survive the fight to come.

Instead, I focused on the feel of him. It was impossible not to. He clouded all of my thoughts.

He stopped walking, giving the kiss everything he had. My head swam and my heart expanded. The new magic inside me ricocheted around, bouncing through my body like fireworks.

By the time he drew away, my head was spinning.

The sound of running footsteps caught my ear, and I looked toward the castle. Rowan and Ana raced toward us, Mayhem flying behind. Chaos and Ruckus trotted alongside, their fangs and horns glinting in the sun.

"I'll take a rain check on that kiss, if you don't mind," I said.

"Aye."

"I can walk."

Slowly, he put me down. My legs wobbled a bit, and flashes of memory burst in my mind—different powers flowing through me, magic tearing me apart and putting me back together. I didn't know how much new power I had, but I seemed to have a lot of it.

Rowan and Ana stopped in front of us, panting.

"Well?" Rowan asked.

"I got it," I said.

"I feel it." Ana's eyes widened. "You are packing some serious heat."

"Thanks. I think."

"It's a good thing," Rowan said. "We'll need it to defeat them."

"Come on." Ana gestured for us to follow. "We need to come up with a plan. And you look like you need some dinner."

My stomach grumbled like it could speak English.

We followed them into the castle, heading straight down to Hans's lair, where the air smelled like baking bread and was warm from the oven.

As if they'd known to expect us, Jude and Hedy were sitting at the table. Ali and Haris were already halfway through bowls of stew, which was no surprise. Thundering footsteps sounded behind us, racing down the stairs.

Caro spilled into the room, platinum hair glinting. "I'm not late, am I?"

"Nope." I took a seat next to Ali, my stomach grumbling at the sight of his stew. The savory scent made my mouth water.

Hans bustled over, a big bowl in his hands. I almost teared up when he put it in front of me.

I looked at him. "You're the most amazing person alive."

He grinned and withdrew his hand from behind his back, presenting me with a tall cup filled with purple liquid. "And your juice!"

I smiled and took it. "Thank you, Hans."

He watched me expectantly, and I sipped the juice. He nodded, satisfied, and turned. Hans really had a thing for juice.

Cade sat next to me, gratefully accepting his own bowl, and everyone else gathered around the table.

"Is it just me, or are we using the kitchen more than the round room these days?" I asked.

"It's not just you," Jude said. "But that's how you know you're onto something big. There's only enough time to eat and talk if you do both at the same time."

Speaking of... I dug into my bowl of stew.

Beef and vegetables, I determined. And it was amazing.

I scarfed it down while Ana and Rowan told an adventurous tale of hiking through the mountains in Nepal to retrieve the three crystals we would use to set our trap and store our power.

Ana finished it by saying, "The crystals are in Hedy's office now."

"I've found a way to transfer your magic to them," Hedy said. "We can perform the spell right before the ambush."

"Perfect," I said. "I have twenty-three and a half hours before Frigg's concealment charm wears off. At that point, I think the Rebel Gods will come for me."

"That gives us time to rally our allies," Ana said.

"We have allies?" I asked.

"The FireSouls, obviously," Ana said.

"Aerdeca and Mordaca," Cade said. "Maybe even the lions that you saved. They like a good fight."

They had a point. We really did have allies. "The Valkyries agreed to fight on our side. I'll have to go get them."

"I can get Oya and her mercenaries," Cade said.

"That'll cost a pretty penny," Haris said.

"They'll give me a discount."

"The Protectorate will help, of course," Jude said. "And I think the ambush should take place in the grove where you hunted Nessie. There's a section there that prohibits transporting. If we can get the gods in there, they can't transport out to escape."

I recalled the section of forest that she was talking about. A clearing about the size of a football field, with thick tree cover all around. "It's perfect."

"Then we have a plan." Rowan smiled. It was thoroughly bloodthirsty. "In twenty-three hours, we'll destroy the Rebel Gods."

An hour later, I returned to Yggdrasil. I wouldn't have expected to be back so soon—especially not when I needed a nap so badly—but I needed to give the Valkyrie the time and location of the final battle. At least this time, I knew exactly how to get here.

It didn't take long to deliver my message, and the Valkyrie promised to come at the appointed time, bringing with them twenty winged warriors.

It would help immensely.

On the way back down the tree, I got even luckier and ran into Ratatoskr. He sat at the base, chomping on acorns and staring at the sky.

His eyes widened as I flew down to him.

"What's that in your hand?" he demanded.

I held out the growler of beer that Cade had sent me with— for just this scenario. I hadn't known if I'd run into Ratatoskr, but if I was going to keep visiting Yggdrasil, it'd be good to have the giant squirrel on my side. At the very least, so he didn't gossip about me.

"Oh this?" I wiggled the jug so he would take it. "It's just your favorite beer."

He gasped and raised a hand to his chest. "For *me*?"

"Of course, silly."

He took it. "Thank you. But what are you doing here?"

"I needed to ask the Valkyrie for help with fighting the Rebel Gods."

He scowled. "No-good toad's bollocks."

"You don't like the Rebel Gods?"

"Of course not. Where is this fight taking place?"

"In a forest in Scotland, twenty hours from now."

His eyes brightened. "Can I come?"

He sounded like he was asking to join me at the fair and he *really* wanted to ride the Ferris wheel. "It'll be dangerous."

He flexed his arms, which were quite puny compared to the rest of him. Then he bared his fangs, which were not. "I like a good fight. And ever since the eagle and Níðhöggr started to get along, there's a lot less to keep me entertained here."

"All right. We'd love to have you. There's a pair of giant lions you'd probably like to meet."

Interest gleamed in his eyes. "Never met lions before."

"You can start tomorrow. And thank you for coming."

He nodded. "I'll follow the Valkyrie and see you there."

We said our goodbyes, and I returned to the Protectorate castle.

14

Nineteen and a half hours later, I flew over the clearing in the woods, watching as my friends and allies arrived to fight. Tension pulled my muscles tight, and nerves kept me moving.

The Protectorate was already here, members stationed in the trees while Hedy prepared the center of the clearing for the spell that would put our magic into the crystals.

Cade's mercenaries had arrived first, led by the African war goddess, Oya. She'd been dressed in fabulous golden armor, and had led her warriors into the woods. They'd melted into the trees and disappeared entirely. I could hear their heartbeats if I really tried, but otherwise, there was neither sight nor sound of them.

Good thing they were on our side.

Aker arrived next, the dual lion god, along with Aerdeca and Mordaca. He prowled the perimeter of the clearing, and I flew down to greet him.

"Thank you for coming."

He inclined his head. "You did me a great favor by releasing me. And I'm going to enjoy my vengeance against those who imprisoned me."

I shivered, the viciousness in his voice making me glad I wasn't his enemy.

Aerdeca and Mordaca were dressed in their usual white and black, respectively, and each wore a tight-fitting jumpsuit and flat-heeled boots, which I had to assume were their fight clothes.

"When does the fun start?" Mordaca grinned, her red lips glinting in the light.

"In thirty minutes, once we've put our magic in the crystals," I said.

Aerdeca whistled. "You are brave."

"No kidding," Mordaca said. "I wouldn't part with my magic for all the money in the world."

"It gives us the advantage we need to win. This way, we determine the timing of the battle and can attack while they're confused. Anyway, if we lose, the Rebel Gods will catch me and kill me. So I'm motivated."

They both nodded, seeming to understand.

Aerdeca hoisted her bow and turned toward the trees. "Well, I'm going to go find a good spot. Best of luck."

Mordaca saluted and followed her.

Cass, Del, and Nix were the next to arrive, along with their significant others, the shifter Aidan, the half demon Roarke, and the vampire Ares. They'd even brought Connor and Claire, their friends and the siblings who ran the coffee shop Potions & Pastilles in Magic's Bend.

I hadn't seen them in ages, but it would be good to have the mercenary, Claire, and the potions master, Connor, on our side.

"We've got your back," Cass said.

"Don't worry," Del added. "You've got this."

I wasn't that confident, but I thanked her anyway. I gave

them each a quick hug, thanked Connor and Claire, and then off they went into the woods, finding their positions to wait.

The Valkyrie were the last to arrive, Ratatoskr in tow. I could hear him complaining about the puny trees, but I only had eyes for Gunnr, the red-haired Valkyrie who gripped a very familiar sword in her hand.

I flew down to greet them, and she held it out. "A gift from Odin."

"My sword?" My heart leapt as I reached for it. The familiar hilt felt like heaven in my hand.

"He felt you might need it."

"I do. I borrowed one, but it's not nearly as good." My mother had given me this sword, and now I would have her with me. She always was, but this was better. "Thank you."

"Of course."

"What is the plan?" Sigrún asked.

I explained about putting my magic into the crystals as bait, and they all whistled. "You are *brave*."

That seemed to be the consensus, but I wasn't sure I agreed. "Once the Rebel Gods arrive, the attack begins. The three of us —you and me, I mean—will fly down and steal the crystals back before they can grab them. By that time, they'll be trapped within the clearing because it's impossible to transport out. We'll take the crystals to my sisters so that we have our magic back, and we'll join the fight."

Gunnr nodded. "I like this plan. Our horses will make us much faster, as well."

After a few more minutes of discussion, the Valkyrie disappeared into the trees.

Hedy approached. "Everything is ready."

I looked toward the center of the clearing, where my sisters waited. "All right."

I walked toward them, my heart pounding. This was it. In

fifteen minutes, Frigg's concealment charm would fade and the Rebel Gods would come.

"Ready?" Ana asked.

"As I'll ever be."

I reached for her hand and Rowan's, squeezing. "I'm sorry about this."

"Don't be," Ana said. "They're hunting all of us. Just because you transitioned first and they're stalking your magic doesn't make this your fault."

"Anyway, I want to take the bastards down," Rowan said.

I nodded. "At least we're together."

"We can do this," Ana said.

"It's now or never," Jude said.

"The magic will take a few minutes." Hedy pointed to the triangle that she'd burned into the earth. "Each of you stand at one of the corners."

We took up our positions, and I stole one last glance at my sisters before focusing on Hedy. My heart thundered as she handed us each a crystal.

They were hollow, each shaped roughly like an egg, and gleamed as if they were made from opal.

"Your magic will go into there," Hedy said. "Be sure to keep a tiny bit for yourself, so that you don't feel the effects of losing your soul. But put most of it into the crystal, which will enhance the signature. That will draw the Rebel Gods, but keep you safe from their attack."

We'd only be without our power for a short while—just long enough for our magic to attract the gods before we could steal it back. Still, the idea was freaking terrifying.

I could see the feeling reflected in Ana and Rowan's faces as well.

I drew in a ragged breath, steadying my breathing. Fear had no place here. I had to be rock solid for this.

In the distance, I caught sight of Cade. He stood next to a tree, his hiding place for the ambush. His eyes were glued to me. I tried to smile at him, drawing strength from his support.

Other than Cade, the forest looked empty. It was silent, save for Hedy's footsteps as she began to pace around us.

"Hold the crystal in both hands," she said. "Envision it as part of yourself."

I did as instructed, but the crystal just felt like a delicate, hollow rock. Not like it was part of me.

Then Hedy raised her wand and magic swelled on the air. She walked behind me and touched it to each of my shoulders, then sprinkled some kind of dust over my head. It smelled of flowers and felt like an electric shock of magic.

Suddenly, the crystal *did* feel like it was part of me. Hedy repeated the ritual to both Ana and Rowan, and their expressions changed as well. Understanding dawned as their gazes dropped to the crystals in their hands.

Hedy's voice buzzed around me, murmuring indistinct words as the crystal vibrated with power. It flowed up my arms, becoming part of me.

"Feed your power into the crystal, saving only a bit for yourself," Hedy said.

It was the most natural thing in the world to follow her orders, so easy to funnel the power from my body into the rock. The magic within me felt like mist, and I pushed it toward the crystal.

Slowly, my limbs weakened and my body felt foggier. Darker. Heavier. It was the strangest feeling, but I kept going, feeding my magic into the crystal.

It began to glow, the opalescent sheen brightening. Rowan and Ana's crystals glowed just as bright.

My head buzzed. Despite the ease of the transformation,

panic threatened at the edges of my mind. It'd been terrible to lose my power months ago. Now, I was willingly giving it away.

The plan. Remember the plan.

It was a good one.

I kept going, feeding the last of my magic into the crystal. I saved just a bit of my healing power and my ability to fly. That way, I could help my friends during the battle.

When the transfer was done, I nearly staggered. Losing my magic felt like hell, but the crystal had become enormously heavy. Rowan and Ana looked pale, and I was sure I looked no better.

Magic radiated out from the crystals, our signatures on steroids. The Norse god Hod had said they had a spell that tracked our signatures—well, they were going to find us *fast* if the signatures were this strong.

"Two minutes left until Frigg's concealment charm fades," Hedy said. "Place the crystals in the center of the triangle."

We did as she commanded, nearly dropping the heavy rocks. As soon as I let go of mine, I went to my knees, gasping.

Ana and Rowan did the same.

"Holy shit, this sucks," Rowan said.

"I feel like I'm going to puke." Ana looked green.

I drew in a ragged breath. Slowly, the illness faded. I staggered to my feet, Ana and Rowan following.

Hedy stepped forward. "When you want to retrieve your magic, put the stone on the ground and stab it with a steel blade to break the crystal."

"Thank you, Hedy," I said.

She nodded. "Now go."

Ana wiped a hand over her brow. "Let's do this."

"Wait." I gave them each a hug. "I love you guys."

"Love you back," they both said.

We drew apart. They both looked better—no longer quite so pale.

We thanked Hedy, then headed off into the forest. They went to the trees, while I flew up to the highest branches, joining Sigrún and Gunnr. They both rode their winged mounts, who'd been enchanted to blend in with the forest. I could still see them, but only because I knew to look.

"Ready?" Sigrún said.

"As I'll ever be." I took a seat on a high tree limb. "Be aware —the crystals are heavy."

"Understood," Gunnr said.

Tension suffused the valley. Endless minutes passed as we waited for the Rebel Gods to arrive. I'd felt Frigg's charm dissipate, so the magic was out there, free as a bird. Ready for the Rebel Gods to find with their spell.

They'd probably found us already and were mustering their troops.

Hopefully, the plan would confuse them enough that we'd have the upper hand. Ana and Rowan weren't sitting ducks. The Rebel Gods would be drawn to their magic, not to them. As long as they didn't catch us all, they wouldn't succeed.

But they didn't show. Not immediately, at least.

Minute after minute passed. I crouched on the tree limb, ready to dart down toward the crystals as soon as they appeared.

When the Rebel Gods arrived, adrenaline shot through my veins. Eleven gods appeared all at once, their power rolling through the clearing. A half second later, demons followed—at least four dozen.

I leapt off the branch, wings flaring, and darted toward the crystals in the middle of the clearing. One of the gods shouted and pointed, confusion in his voice.

Behind me, I heard the Valkyrie on their horses.

The rest of my friends and allies launched their attack,

bursting from the trees and providing us with cover as we flew for the crystals.

In the chaos, it took the gods a moment to figure out what was going on. Most didn't notice the crystals. But Eris did. She pointed and shouted, and the rest charged.

Once it became clear where they were headed, flame burst up around the crystals. Claire, Cass's friend, had used her fire magic to create the barrier as we'd planned. It flared tall and bright, a barrier that I prayed would work.

Eris was twenty feet away from the crystals. The others were fighting. We would make it in time.

The Valkyrie's mounts shrieked in fear. I glanced back, seeing them wheeling away from the gods below. Something had frightened them!

They were supposed to be okay with fire. One of the Rebel Gods?

Sigrún and Gunnr's panicked eyes met mine as they tried to control their mounts.

Shit!

It was up to me to save the crystals.

I flew toward them as fast as I could, my lungs and muscles burning. Eris was nearly to the fire barrier, only ten feet away. The fire flamed high, but the gods were crazy.

The crystals were so heavy. Could I carry them all?

I had to try.

I swept down and grabbed the three crystals, heaving them off the ground. I darted away.

A bolt of fire blasted toward me and I dived, moving slowly because of the weight of my cargo. The flames plowed into my left wing, making me spin in the air.

I fumbled the rocks, dropping one.

Mine.

It plunged to the ground, right in the middle of the triangle of flame. *Shit!*

But I was close to Rowan and Ana. They needed their magic. I prayed that the flame would protect my crystal as I dived into the trees.

Behind me, the sound of battle raged. The lions' roars tore through the air, and Ratatoskr's battle cry of "To victory and acorns!" followed.

I spotted Rowan and Ana right where they said they'd be, at the base of an oak tree with two trunks. They looked up to me, relief and horror painted on their faces in equal measure.

I hurled their crystals at them, and they caught them handily, threw them to the ground, and smashed them with their swords.

Purple smoke rose up from the broken rocks, flowing into Ana and Rowan, returning their magic to them.

I gave them one last look, then whirled, racing back toward the clearing. I caught sight of Ratatoskr tearing demons apart left and right. He looked like a kid on Christmas morning, tearing open presents. Except he was tearing open demons, and blood was spraying like wrapping paper and ribbon.

Connor, the potion master, hurled potion bombs from his perch in one of the trees, hitting the demon mercenaries with deadly aim. His sister, Claire, joined Cass in an attack against a blue god who seemed to control ice. Both women fought ice with fire, hurling their flame with deadly accuracy.

Caro, Ali, and Haris fought alongside Jude against the god in the brown robe, while Aker, the dual lion god, fought a god shaped like a massive snake. Was that what had scared the Valkyrie's horses?

Sigrún and Gunnr had abandoned their mounts, likely letting them return to Yggdrasil, and flew toward Hod, the Norse god. He battled the other Valkyrie, who seemed determined to take down the traitor. He might be blind, but he was so fast I could hardly see him move. Oya's mercenaries picked off the demons.

The rest of my friends fought demons and gods, while Cade squared off against Hum Hau, the Mayan god of death. He fought in wolf form, tearing at Hum Hau, who flickered with a light that made him look like a skeleton.

My gaze went unerringly toward the flame that still surrounded my crystal, praying to anyone who would listen. *Let me find it before they get it.*

I spotted it just in time to see Eris—inside the ring of flame. She was so crazy that she'd run through the three-foot thick wall of fire. All her hair was gone and her dress flaming.

She laughed maniacally as she smashed my crystal on the ground and inhaled the purple smoke.

No!

My wings faltered, and I nearly fell from the sky.

Eris had taken my magic.

Her laugh was a crazed sound that shot through me like ice. Lightning began to strike, thunder cracking through the air and making my eardrums feel like they were bleeding.

Shit. She was using my magic.

I had to kill her. She couldn't escape with it. Even if I never got it back—grief tore through me at the idea—I couldn't let her have it. The damage she could do...

Maybe I'd played this all wrong. I shouldn't have left my magic behind, but I hadn't been able to abandon my sisters like that.

The fight raged around me as Eris's lightning crashed all around. It lit up trees and fried bushes. Fortunately, her aim wasn't any good. Not yet, at least. All she needed was a little practice.

I drew my mother's sword and charged her, knowing that I was dreadfully outmatched. But at least I had my wings.

Wind tore at my hair as I hurtled downward, approaching her from behind. She seemed to sense me, turning just as I struck out with my blade.

I pierced her in the shoulder, and she shrieked, her eyes widening. The blood that poured from her new wound matched the stuff streaking down her face.

Mayhem appeared, blasting her with fire, then whirled away and flew into the trees. Smart dog.

She hissed and threw out her hand, hitting me with a sonic boom that sent me hurtling through the air and slamming into a tree.

Pain flared as my mind scrambled to process.

How the hell did she get *that* power?

I thought it was gone.

Talk about insult to injury.

Rage shot through me, overcoming the ache in my middle. It felt like my insides had been liquefied, but I ignored it. I staggered to my feet, catching sight of the torn-apart body of the Mayan god.

Cade had really done a number on him.

My gaze darted through the clearing. In his wolf form, he charged Eris, dodging one of her lightning bolts and leaping toward her with his mouth open, fangs glinting in the light. He bit her arm and spun her around, but she hit him with a sonic boom, sending him flying.

I leapt into the air, aching wings carrying me toward Eris.

As if she'd heard me—hell, she probably did, with Heimdall's power—she turned and thrust out her hand.

Thunder cracked, and I looked up. Lightning flashed in the sky, and I dived, barely avoiding it. I raced toward her, slicing out with my blade and hitting her in the arm.

She shrieked, and I flew up, racing away.

In the distance, Cade fought another god who had ambushed him right after Eris had hit him with the sonic boom. I could see the desperation in his movements, the desire to get back to Eris and take her out.

Adrenaline raced through me as I whirled to head back down to Eris. The clearing was a madhouse, with enemies and allies going at it full tilt.

I raised my sword, determined to make this the kill shot.

Then light and pain flared through me, accompanied by the crack of thunder. I never saw the lightning coming. It hurtled from the sky, crashing into the ground with a thud that was sickening.

Every muscle and bone in my body ached like hell. The trees above me spun like I was on a carnival ride.

I turned my head, catching sight of Cass sprawled out next to me. Blood seeped from a wound at her neck, mixing with her red hair.

Panic flared.

Aching, I dragged myself to my hands and knees and crawled to her.

"Cass!" I cried.

She blinked, eyes cloudy with pain. The wound at her neck was atrocious—I'd never seen anything so terrible. How was she even alive?

Fear doused me in ice water. *She was dying.*

"Bree," she croaked.

Oh god, this had been a terrible plan.

A roar of fear and pain sounded in the distance, but I ignored it, thrusting my hands onto Cass's chest and giving her every bit of healing power I had in me.

Thank fates this was the power I'd saved.

My arms shook as I forced the magic into her. The wound at

her neck began to close, but it was too slow. I was stopping the flow of blood and mending the skin, but it might not be enough.

Tears pricked at my eyes.

I kept giving her my magic, but it was flagging. My healing gift wasn't strong enough. Not with a wound this grievous.

This cost was too great.

I'd screwed this up so bad.

A huge man fell to his knees on the other side of Cass, grief and fear all over his face. His auburn hair was flecked with blood, as was his face.

Aidan. Her boyfriend.

"Cass!"

I'd never heard such pain in a sound.

He touched the side of her neck on the only undamaged spot.

Immediately, she glowed with light. The wound began to close, faster than I had managed.

Aidan had healing powers!

Relief surged through me.

Within seconds, the wound was gone. Cass sat up, her color returned. Aidan sagged, weakened from the effort. He must have given her everything.

"Go!" Cass yelled. She kissed him quickly, then pushed him away.

He grabbed her and kissed her back, hard and fast, then sprinted back to the battle, transforming into a griffon as he ran. He was massive, a terrifying beast with golden feathers and fur and a beak that could crush cows. He launched himself into the air, then whirled around to return to the fight.

Cass looked at me, fully healed. "Eris took your magic."

"Yeah. We have to kill her."

"We'll do more than that." Cass staggered to her feet. "We'll get your magic back for you."

"How?"

She raised a hand and wiggled her fingers. "FireSoul. I've never given magic to another, but we're going to try. I'll take it from her and give it to you."

Hope flared in my chest. "How?"

"You deliver the killing blow. Then I'll get to work."

"I can do that."

We turned, searching for Eris.

Horror streaked through me as I caught sight of Rowan and Ana racing for her, anger and determination on their faces.

Ana was supposed to be gone.

"Come on!" I launched myself into the air and flew for Eris.

All around, the battle raged, but I only had eyes for her. She was getting better with her lightning bolts, but I dodged every one, determination fueling me.

I might get my power back.

From the far side of the clearing, Del shot an enormous icicle right at Eris. It flew through the air, sparkling and bright, but Eris didn't notice it.

The spear pierced her through the thigh, throwing her to the ground. She shrieked, pure rage and agony in the sound.

I dived low, just as Rowan and Ana neared. I struck out with my blade, slicing at Eris's neck. Ana threw a dagger, hitting Eris in the eye. Rowan went for the heart, plunging her blade deep.

The goddess thrashed, and the sight turned my stomach.

But it had to be done. What she would do with my magic was too terrible to contemplate.

Cass joined us, falling to her knees by Eris's body. "She won't stay down long."

I had to agree. Eris was too strong to allow a little thing like three mortal wounds to keep her down.

"Guard us!" Cass said. "I'll need a minute, at least."

Ana turned, throwing out her hands and creating a massive

white dome over our heads. Her magic crackled and popped, the white shield growing more opaque as she gave it everything she had.

Cass reached for my hand, and I grabbed hers. "Focus on the magic."

I did as she commanded while she put her other hand on Eris's chest.

The goddess twitched, trying to get up, but Cass pushed her down.

White flame flickered around Cass's arm, reaching down to Eris's body. Cass winced, her face twisting with pain, but kept the flame going.

Eris hissed, and her magic flared. It felt like acid against my skin and smelled like putrid wounds. She was as dark as they came.

Cass's magic competed with hers, a much purer signature that smelled like fresh water and sounded like rustling leaves.

When the flame crept from Cass's arm across her body and into me, the burning began. I gritted my teeth and ignored it, praying that Cass's magic would work.

The burning grew worse, making sweat drip down my temples, but magic came with it.

My magic.

It flowed into me, strong and fierce. Filling me like a well. Strength flowed through my muscles as the power returned to its rightful home.

Beside me, Cass sagged, her strength clearly waning. Eris looked worse, though. Blood poured from her wounds, and her skin turned gray.

Finally, the last of the magic flowed from her into me. Cass dropped her hands and sagged, panting. Eris's body shriveled into dust.

I sucked in a deep breath, feeling like a million bucks. "Are you okay, Cass?"

"Fine." Her voice sounded weak, though.

I touched her shoulder, feeding some healing energy into her. Now that I had the rest of my magic—including a bit of the healing power I'd put into the crystal—it was stronger. Soon, she looked good as new.

She grinned. "Thanks."

"No, thank you." What she'd done for me was enormous. But now wasn't the time to dwell on it. The fight wasn't over yet. I looked at Ana, who still had her back to us. "Drop the shield, Ana!"

She did it immediately, turning, her gaze searching for me.

"I'm okay!" I shouted.

She nodded, then sprinted for the trees, no doubt to recoup and restart the fight from a position of power. She'd always fought smart.

I shot toward the sky, the magic filling me to bursting.

A quick survey of the clearing showed many of my friends wounded. But many more of the enemies were down. There were still five gods standing, and Cocidius was one of them.

He hurled a dagger at me, and I dived, barely avoiding the gleaming silver spike that sped toward me. I didn't see the second blade, however, and it pierced me in the shoulder. I spun backward, my wings faltering.

Agony flared as I managed to right myself and yank the blade from my shoulder. Each beat of my wing tore through me, but I dragged my mind away from the pain.

I needed to end this. If it kept going, we'd lose our advantage. We already might have, given how weak my friends were looking. Magic was depleted and wounds were fierce.

I flew high, reaching inside myself for my new magic. But I

had to be smart. I might have a dozen different powers, but I only had so much juice. I couldn't waste it.

I didn't even know what all I had, but I needed to find a way to give my friends the advantage, at least.

The hot crackle of lightning burned in my chest.

I could work with that.

I reached for the lightning that was becoming so familiar, building five massive lightning bolts. It took everything I had in me to create the five bolts, and I knew the bolts would only stun the Rebel Gods for a moment.

But if I could weaken them...

They cracked from the sky in unison, the thunder shaking my bones. Each bolt hit a god, sending them flying to their backs.

My friends took advantage, racing toward the weakened gods, who were already rising to their feet. If the other gods and mercenaries hadn't been killed already, I never would have managed.

As a wolf, Cade lunged toward Cocidius, his jaws open. He tore at the god's throat. Aker went for another god, while Mordaca and Aerdeca joined the FireSouls in their attack. Ratatoskr lunged toward another, Jude at his side.

Ana and Rowan went for the god in the brown robes, Caro at their side. They fell on him like berserkers, their blades flying. I hurtled down to join them, not wanting to leave my sisters without help.

I stabbed my blade through the god's throat, but there was every chance he was already dead. For good measure, Mayhem appeared, blasting him with fire.

We stumbled back from the body.

All around, the sound of heaving breaths filled the air.

The Rebel Gods were dead.

Relief rushed through me, and I sagged, my wings drooped.

Was it really over?

In a swirl of golden light, Cade shifted into his human form. He raced for me, his clothes and skin covered in blood. I threw myself at him, wrapping my arms around his neck.

"I'm so glad you're okay," I mumbled against him. Every ounce of magic had drained from me, leaving me exhausted and aching.

"You have your magic back?" he asked.

"I do." I pulled away, turning to inspect the rest of the clearing. I needed to know if anyone had died.

My friends staggered around, clutching wounds and looking pretty damned bad. Aerdeca's white suit was covered in blood, and the FireSouls looked like hell. But no one was dead, at least. Even the mercenaries all looked fine.

Every body on the ground belonged to a demon. Mayhem flew through the clearing, inspecting every charred and dead demon.

Anyone with transport powers was evacuating the seriously wounded, but there were no tears of grief in the group. What a miracle that was.

Thank fates we were all okay.

I staggered finally, going to my knees.

Apparently, adrenaline had kept me going. And now that the threat had passed and no one appeared to be dead, standing was above my pay grade.

"Are you okay?" Cade asked.

"I'll be fine. Just let me sit a moment."

Ana and Rowan joined me, collapsing next to me and panting.

"We did it," Ana said.

"They're *dead.*" The vicious joy in Rowan's voice made me smile. Sure, it was a bit weird. But so were our lives. And if anyone had reason to be happy that the Rebel Gods were gone, it was Rowan.

"Thank fates for that," I said. "We're safe."

And together. Finally, after five years apart and fifteen years of running and hiding, we'd defeated our hunters. We'd avenged our mother.

And we were safe.

EPILOGUE

T*hree days later*

The party at the Whisky and Warlock was heaving. The Protectorate had booked the whole place for the night, which was apparently normal when a person advanced from trainee to full member.

I stood with my sisters, pressed in with the rest of the crowd. Jude stood on a chair in the corner, the fireplace flickering to her left. She raised her glass. We all followed suit, except me. I kept my pink cocktail—the Destroyer of Rebel Gods, it'd been named—lowered. I was pretty sure this toast was for me, and while I wasn't up to date on my etiquette, even I knew it was bad taste to toast yourself.

"To Bree!" Jude said. "Who advanced through the training program in record time, largely due to the fact that she fought the most fearsome enemy on earth and won."

"Which should have been impossible!" Hedy grinned. "And those words came directly from Arach."

Jude turned to me. "Welcome to the PITs."

I grinned and laughed. I'd chosen to join Caro, Ali, and Haris on the Paranormal Investigative Team. The three of them cheered wildly, and the rest of the crowd joined in. My friends clinked their glasses together and shouted congratulations.

I sipped my drink, lowering it in time for Caro, Ali, and Haris to rush me and give me a hug.

"Welcome to the team!" Caro said.

"It'll be a blast," Ali added.

Haris grinned. "I can't wait for you to show us up."

I laughed. "I can't wait for the first day of work."

They grinned and stayed to chat for a few minutes, then left to refill their drinks.

Ana leaned against my side. "Not bad, sis."

"Thanks."

Rowan hugged me from the side. She still hadn't figured out what was wrong with her magic, but she was adjusting better to life here. Though she was still jumpy and slightly obsessed with becoming a weapons master to make up for her magical short-comings, she wasn't nearly as haunted looking as she had been before we'd defeated the Rebel Gods three days ago. It was like a weight had lifted off her shoulders.

Music blasted through the crowded room, and Mayhem shot into the air, doing loop-de-loops to "I Would Walk 500 Miles." She loved The Proclaimers, apparently.

On the bar, Boris ate a bowl of peanuts. He sat with Ratatoskr, who'd magically shrunk down for the occasion. He didn't necessarily like being smaller—very grumpy, that rodent —but he'd wanted to attend the party and this was the only way he'd fit in the building. He'd wanted to be human size at least, but we'd explained that he couldn't walk through Edinburgh like that. It wasn't true, but we were afraid we couldn't afford his bar bill if he wasn't tiny. The Valkyrie said he could drink them all under the table. And that was when they were drinking as a team. This way, he got to drink all the beer he wanted, and it was dirt cheap.

He hadn't said no to that, at least.

Cass, Del, and Nix pushed their way through the crowd to join us. They'd come to celebrate, and their boyfriends leaned against the wall near the windows, drinking Scotch and chatting with Cade. It was all very manly looking, and I vastly preferred my own pink drink. Destroyer of Rebel Gods. Scotch couldn't boast a name like that.

"Thanks for coming!" I said.

"We wanted to congratulate you." Cass thrust a package into my hand. It was wrapped in brown paper and looked like a five-year-old had done it. She grinned. "Wrapped it myself!"

"Thanks!" I pulled off the paper to reveal three rings set with large white stones.

"They're lightstone rings," Nix said. "One for each of you, actually."

"They'll light up whenever you need them to," Del added. "Really handy."

"And really hard to find," I said. "I've heard of them. They're rare. Thank you."

Ana and Rowan took their rings, then hugged the FireSouls.

I did the same. "Thank you again for your help with the Rebel Gods."

"Anytime." Cass grinned. "We always like a good fight."

"You almost died."

"It was a *really* good fight," she said. "And you saved me."

"Aidan did."

"Only because of you. I wouldn't have made it long enough for him to find me."

Thank fates I'd held on to my healing power, then. "We couldn't have done it without you. Truly."

"You helped us once," Nix said. "We're glad to do the same."

We talked for a few more minutes, but I caught sight of Cade coming toward me from the bar. He'd left the other men, and if the pink-filled glass in his hand was any indication, he'd made a detour on his way over here to get me another drink.

The others seemed to notice my distraction, and made their goodbyes.

Whoops.

Rowan and Ana melted into the crowd, smiling at me and shooting me a thumbs-up. Mayhem hovered over their heads.

Cade stopped at my side, handing me the drink.

"Thanks." I set my empty on the table, took the glass, and sipped appreciatively.

I leaned against him, enjoying the sight of the crowd. It was as natural as breathing to lean against him, and I knew I'd found something good. Really good. And permanent.

He reached for my hand and gripped it.

I smiled. "I'm glad we found each other."

"Aye, me too." He pressed a kiss to my forehead. "And I'm glad the Protectorate found you."

"Me too." I could already tell I was going to be happy here. With the Rebel Gods gone and my sisters at my side, we had a real life ahead of us. We just had to figure out what kind of Dragon Gods Rowan and Ana were. No doubt that would come with its own set of challenges, but we were ready for them.

No question.

THANK YOU FOR READING!

I hope you enjoyed *Master of Magic*. Reviews are *so* helpful to authors. If you want to leave one, you can do so on Amazon or GoodReads.

Join my mailing list at www.linseyhall.com/subscribe to stay updated. You'll also get a free ebook copy of *Hidden Magic*. The story stars Cass, Del, and Nix, the FireSouls who help Bree in the final battle of this book.

Turn the page for an excerpt of *Hidden Magic*.

EXCERPT OF HIDDEN MAGIC

Jungle, Southeast Asia
   Five years before the events in Ancient Magic

"How much are we being paid for this job again?" I glanced at the dudes filling the bar. It was a motley crowd of supernaturals, many of whom looked shifty as hell.

"Not nearly enough for one as dangerous as this." Del frowned at the man across the bar, who was giving her his best sexy face. There was a lot of eyebrow movement happening. "Is he having a seizure?"

"Looks like it." Nix grinned. "Though I gotta say, I wasn't expecting this. We're basically in a tree, for magic's sake. In the middle of the jungle! Where are all these dudes coming from?"

"According to my info, there's a mining operation near here. Though I'd say we're more *under* a tree than *in* a tree."

"I'm with Cass," Del said. "Under, not in."

"Fair enough," Nix said.

We were deep in Southeast Asia, in a bar that had long ago

been reclaimed by the jungle. A massive fig tree had grown over and around the ancient building, its huge roots strangling the stone walls. It was straight out of a fairy tale.

Monks had once lived here, but a few supernaturals of indeterminate species had gotten ahold of it and turned it into a watering hole for the local supernaturals. We were meeting our contact here, but he was late.

"Hey, pretty lady." A smarmy voice sounded from my left. "What are you?"

I turned to face the guy who was giving me the up and down, his gaze roving from my tank top to my shorts. He wasn't Clarence, our local contact. And if he meant "what kind of supernatural are you?" I sure as hell wouldn't be answering. That could get me killed.

"Not interested is what I am," I said.

"Aww, that's no way to treat a guy." He grabbed my hip, rubbed his thumb up and down.

I smacked his hand away, tempted to throat-punch him. It was my favorite move, but I didn't want to start a fight before Clarence got here. Didn't want to piss off our boss.

The man raised his hands. "Hey, hey. No need to get feisty. You three sisters?"

I glanced at Nix and Del, at their dark hair that was so different from my red. We were all about twenty, but we looked nothing alike. And while we might call ourselves sisters—*deirfiúr* in our native Irish—this idiot didn't know that.

"Go away." I had no patience for dirt bags who touched me without asking. "Run along and flirt with your hand, because that's all the action you'll be getting tonight."

His face turned a mottled red, and he raised a fist. His magic welled, the scent of rotten fruit overwhelming.

He thought he was going to smack me? Or use his magic against me?

Ha.

I lashed out, punching him in the throat. His eyes bulged and he gagged. I kneed him in the crotch, grinning when he keeled over.

"Hey!" A burly man with a beard lunged for us, his buddy beside him following. "That's no way—"

"To treat a guy?" I finished for him as I kicked out at him. My tall, heavy boots collided with his chest, sending him flying backward. I never used my magic—didn't want to go to jail and didn't want to blow things up—but I sure as hell could fight.

His friend raised his hand and sent a blast of wind at us. It threw me backward, sending me skidding across the floor.

By the time I'd scrambled to my feet, a brawl had broken out in the bar. Fists flew left and right, with a bit of magic thrown in. Nothing bad enough to ruin the bar, like jets of flame, because no one wanted to destroy the only watering hole for a hundred miles, but enough that it lit up the air with varying magical signatures.

Nix conjured a baseball bat and swung it at a burly guy who charged her, while Del teleported behind a horned demon and smashed a chair over his head. I'd always been jealous of Del's ability to sneak up on people like that.

All in all, it was turning into a good evening. A fight between supernaturals was fun.

"Enough!" the bartender bellowed. "Or no more beer!"

The patrons quieted immediately. Fights might be fun, but they weren't worth losing beer over.

I glared at the jerk who'd started it. There was no way I'd take the blame, even though I'd thrown the first punch. He should have known better.

The bartender gave me a look and I shrugged, hiking a thumb at the jerk who'd touched me. "He shoulda kept his hands to himself."

"Fair enough," the bartender said.

I nodded and turned to find Nix and Del. They'd grabbed our beers and were putting them on a table in the corner. I went to join them.

We were a team. Sisters by choice, ever since we'd woken in a field at fifteen with no memories other than those that said we were FireSouls on the run from someone who had hurt us. Who was hunting us.

Our biggest goal, even bigger than getting out from under our current boss's thumb, was to save enough money to buy concealment charms that would hide us from the monster who hunted us. He was just a shadowy memory, but it was enough to keep us running.

"Where is Clarence, anyway?" I pulled my damp tank top away from my sweaty skin. The jungle was damned hot. We couldn't break into the temple until Clarence gave us the information we needed to get past the guard at the front. And we didn't need to spend too much longer in this bar.

Del glanced at her watch, her blue eyes flashing with annoyance. "He's twenty minutes late. Old Man Bastard said he should be here at eight."

Old Man Bastard—OMB for short—was our boss. His name said it all. Del, Nix, and I were FireSouls, the most despised species of supernatural because we could steal other magical being's powers if we killed them. We'd never done that, of course, but OMB didn't care. He'd figured out our secret when we were too young to hide it effectively and had been blackmailing us to work for him ever since.

It'd been four years of finding and stealing treasure on his behalf. Treasure hunting was our other talent, a gift from the dragon with whom legend said we shared a soul. No one had seen a dragon in centuries, so I wasn't sure if the legend was even true, but dragons were covetous, so it made sense they had a knack for finding treasure.

"What are we after again?" Nix asked.

"A pair of obsidian daggers," Del said. "Nice ones."

"And how much is this job worth?" Nix repeated my earlier question. Money was always on our minds. It was our only chance at buying our freedom, but OMB didn't pay us enough for it to be feasible anytime soon. We kept meticulous track of our earnings and saved like misers anyway.

"A thousand each."

"Damn, that's pathetic." I slouched back in my chair and stared up at the ceiling, too bummed about our crappy pay to even be impressed by the stonework and vines above my head.

"Hey, pretty ladies." The oily voice made my skin crawl. We just couldn't get a break in here. I looked up to see Clarence, our contact.

Clarence was a tall man, slender as a vine, and had the slicked back hair and pencil-thin mustache of a 1940s movie star. Unfortunately, it didn't work on him. Probably because his stare was like a lizard's. He was more Gomez Addams than Clark Gable. I'd bet anything that he liked working for OMB.

"Hey, Clarence," I said. "Pull up a seat and tell us how to get into the temple."

Clarence slid into a chair, his movement eerily snakelike. I shivered and scooted my chair away, bumping into Del. The scent of her magic flared, a clean hit of fresh laundry, as she no doubt suppressed her instinct to transport away from Clarence. If I had her gift of teleportation, I'd have to repress it as well.

"How about a drink first?" Clarence said.

Del growled, but Nix interjected, her voice almost nice. She had the most self control out of the three of us. "No can do, Clarence. You know... Mr. Oribis"—her voice tripped on the name, probably because she wanted to call him OMB—"wants the daggers soon. Maybe next time, though."

"Next time." Clarence shook his head like he didn't believe her. He might be a snake, but he was a clever one. His chest puffed up a bit. "You know I'm the only one who knows how to get into the temple. How to get into any of the places in this jungle."

"And we're so grateful you're meeting with us. Mr. Oribis is so grateful." Nix dug into her pocket and pulled out the crumpled envelope that contained Clarence's pay. We'd counted it and found—unsurprisingly—that it was more than ours combined, even though all he had to do was chat with us for two minutes. I'd wanted to scream when I'd seen it.

Clarence's gaze snapped to the money. "All right, all right."

Apparently his need to be flattered went out the window when cash was in front of his face. Couldn't blame him, though. I was the same way.

"So, what are we up against?" I asked.

The temple containing the daggers had been built by supernaturals over a thousand years ago. Like other temples of its kind, it was magically protected. Clarence's intel would save us a ton of time and damage to the temple if we could get around the enchantments rather than breaking through them.

"Dvarapala. A big one."

"A gatekeeper?" I'd seen one of the giant, stone monster statues at another temple before.

"Yep." He nodded slowly. "Impossible to get through. The temple's as big as the Titanic—hidden from humans, of course —but no one's been inside in centuries, they say."

Hidden from humans was a given. They had no idea supernaturals existed, and we wanted to keep it that way.

"So how'd you figure out the way in?" Del asked. "And why

haven't you gone in? Bet there's lots of stuff you could fence in there. Temples are usually full of treasure."

"A bit of pertinent research told me how to get in. And I'd rather sell the entrance information and save my hide. It won't be easy to get past the booby traps in there."

Hide? Snakeskin, more like. Though he had a point. I didn't think he'd last long trying to get through a temple on his own.

"So? Spill it," I said, anxious to get going.

He leaned in, and the overpowering scent of cologne and sweat hit me. I grimaced, held my breath, then leaned forward to hear his whispers.

As soon as Clarence walked away, the communications charms around my neck vibrated. I jumped, then groaned. Only one person had access to this charm.

I shoved the small package Clarence had given me into my short's pocket and pressed my fingertips to the comms charm, igniting its magic.

"Hello, Mr. Oribis." I swallowed my bile at having to be polite.

"Girls," he grumbled.

Nix made a gagging face. We hated when he called us girls.

"Change of plans. You need to go to the temple tonight."

"What? But it's dark. We're going tomorrow." He never changed the plans on us. This was weird.

"I need the daggers sooner. Go tonight."

My mind raced. "The jungle is more dangerous in the dark. We'll do it if you pay us more."

"Twice the usual," Del said.

A tinny laugh echoed from the charm. "Pay *you* more? You're lucky I pay you at all."

I gritted my teeth and said, "But we've been working for you for four years without a raise."

"And you'll be working for me for four more years. And four after that. And four after that." Annoyance lurked in his tone. So did his low opinion of us.

Del's and Nix's brows crinkled in distress. We'd always suspected that OMB wasn't planning to let us buy our freedom, but he'd dangled that carrot in front of us. What he'd just said made that seem like a big fat lie, though. One we could add to the many others he'd told us.

An urge to rebel, to stand up to the bully who controlled our lives, seethed in my chest.

"No," I said. "You treat us like crap, and I'm sick of it. Pay us fairly."

"I treat you like *crap,* as you so eloquently put it, because that is exactly what you are. *FireSouls.*" He spit the last word, imbuing it with so much venom I thought it might poison me.

I flinched, frantically glancing around to see if anyone in the bar had heard what he'd called us. Fortunately, they were all distracted. That didn't stop my heart from thundering in my ears as rage replaced the fear. I opened my mouth to shout at him, but snapped it shut. I was too afraid of pissing him off.

"Get it by dawn," he barked. "Or I'm turning one of you in to the Order of the Magica. Prison will be the least of your worries. They might just execute you."

I gasped. "You wouldn't." Our government hunted and imprisoned—or destroyed—FireSouls.

"Oh, I would. And I'd enjoy it. The three of you have been more trouble than you're worth. You're getting cocky, thinking you have a say in things like this. Get the daggers by dawn, or one of you ends up in the hands of the Order."

My skin chilled, and the floor felt like it had dropped out from under me. He was serious.

"Fine." I bit off the end of the word, barely keeping my voice from shaking. "We'll do it tonight. Del will transport them to you as soon as we have them."

"Excellent." Satisfaction rang in his tone, and my skin crawled. "Don't disappoint me, or you know what will happen."

The magic in the charm died. He'd broken the connection.

I collapsed back against the chair. In times like these, I wished I had it in me to kill. Sure, I offed demons when they came at me on our jobs, but that was easy because they didn't actually die. Killing their earthly bodies just sent them back to their hell.

But I couldn't kill another supernatural. Not even OMB. It might get us out of this lifetime of servitude, but I didn't have it in me. And what if I failed? I was too afraid of his rage—and the consequences—if I didn't succeed.

"Shit, shit, shit." Nix's green eyes were stark in her pale face. "He means it."

"Yeah." Del's voice shook. "We need to get those daggers."

"Now," I said.

"I wish I could just conjure a forgery," Nix said. "I really don't want to go out into the jungle tonight. Getting past the Dvara-pala in the dark will suck."

Nix was a conjurer, able to create almost anything using just her magic. Massive or complex things, like airplanes or guns, were outside of her ability, but a couple of daggers wouldn't be hard.

Trouble was, they were a magical artifact, enchanted with the ability to return to whoever had thrown them. Like boomerangs. Though Nix could conjure the daggers, we couldn't enchant them.

"We need to go. We only have six hours until dawn." I grabbed my short swords from the table and stood, shoving them into the holsters strapped to my back.

A hush descended over the crowded bar.

I stiffened, but the sound of the staticky TV in the corner made me relax. They weren't interested in me. Just the news, which was probably being routed through a dozen techno-witches to get this far into the jungle.

The grave voice of the female reporter echoed through the quiet bar. "The FireSoul was apprehended outside of his apartment in Magic's Bend, Oregon. He is currently in the custody of the Order of the Magica, and his trial is scheduled for tomorrow morning. My sources report that execution is possible."

I stifled a crazed laugh. Perfect timing. Just what we needed to hear after OMB's threat. A reminder of what would happen if he turned us into the Order of the Magica. The hush that had descended over the previously rowdy crowd—the kind of hush you get at the scene of a big accident—indicated what an interesting freaking topic this was. FireSouls were the bogeymen. *I* was the bogeyman, even though I didn't use my powers. But as long as no one found out, we were safe.

My gaze darted to Del and Nix. They nodded toward the door. It was definitely time to go.

As the newscaster turned her report toward something more boring and the crowd got rowdy again, we threaded our way between the tiny tables and chairs.

I shoved the heavy wooden door open and sucked in a breath of sticky jungle air, relieved to be out of the bar. Night creatures screeched, and moonlight filtered through the trees above. The jungle would be a nice place if it weren't full of things that wanted to kill us.

"We're never escaping him, are we?" Nix said softly.

"We will." Somehow. Someday. "Let's just deal with this for now."

We found our motorcycles, which were parked in the lot

with a dozen other identical ones. They were hulking beasts with massive, all-terrain tires meant for the jungle floor. We'd done a lot of work in Southeast Asia this year, and these were our favored forms of transportation in this part of the world.

Del could transport us, but it was better if she saved her power. It wasn't infinite, though it did regenerate. But we'd learned a long time ago to save Del's power for our escape. Nothing worse than being trapped in a temple with pissed off guardians and a few tripped booby traps.

We'd scouted out the location of the temple earlier that day, so we knew where to go.

I swung my leg over Secretariat—I liked to name my vehicles —and kicked the clutch. The engine roared to life. Nix and Del followed, and we peeled out of the lot, leaving the dingy yellow light of the bar behind.

Our headlights illuminated the dirt road as we sped through the night. Huge fig trees dotted the path on either side, their twisted trunks and roots forming an eerie corridor. Elephant-ear sized leaves swayed in the wind, a dark emerald that gleamed in the light.

Jungle animals howled, and enormous lightning bugs flitted along the path. They were too big to be regular bugs, so they were most likely some kind of fairy, but I wasn't going to stop to investigate. There were dangerous creatures in the jungle at night—one of the reasons we hadn't wanted to go now—and in our world, fairies could be considered dangerous.

Especially if you called them lightning bugs.

A roar sounded in the distance, echoing through the jungle and making the leaves rustle on either side as small animals scurried for safety.

The roar came again, only closer.

Then another, and another.

"Oh shit," I muttered. This was bad.

~~~

Join my mailing list to get a free copy of *Hidden Magic.* No spam and you can leave anytime!

AUTHOR'S NOTE

Thanks for reading *Master of Magic!* The author's note is where I normally talk about the history and mythology in the book, and *Master of Magic* had plenty of it.

There are quite a few historical and mythological references in *Master of Magic.* To start, the guards of the Rebel Gods realm come from myth. Janus is the two headed god from Roman mythology who presides over beginnings and transitions, as well as gates and doors. Aker is an Egyptian god who is actually two lions. In some depictions, he is a strip of land with two heads at each end, facing away from each other. He is a protective deity and a gatekeeper.

The different realms in the Rebel Gods headquarters are from mythology—Roman, Mayan, Hindu, and others. The Hindu god was Agni, the fire god, while the Mayan god was Hum Hau, the god of death.

One of the most impressive places is the House of Wisdom, which was an enormous library located in Baghdad. It was one of the most prominent intellectual centers during the Islamic Golden Age (8th - 13th Centuries AD) and was built by Abbasid Caliph Hard al-Rashid in the late 8th Century AD. It was a particularly cool place because scholars from many backgrounds could visit to use it, including those of Jewish and Christian faith. The House of Wisdom was destroyed during the siege of Baghdad in 1258, which is such a tragedy that I had the terrible Rebel Gods do one good deed and save it.

One of my favorite parts to write was Bree's return visit to Yggdrasil. There is so much information available about Norse myth and stories that I was able to use a lot of it, and in some cases, put my own spin on it. One cool thing was Mia, the game that Cade plays with Ratatoskr. It was a real Viking gambling game that relied on people lying about their dice tosses. In some cases, the game could turn deadly if your bluff was caught.

Hliðskjálf was the throne that Odin and Freya sat upon. In myth, it it his throne alone, and it allows him to see the entire kingdom. When Bree travels around Yggdrasil using the different portals, they are all different from the regular portals on earth. One of them gleamed like a rainbow, and it was meant to represent the rainbow bridge that connects Midgard (earth) and Asgard, the realm of the Aesir gods.

Mímir was in fact a wise man and Jotunn who lived in a well that was associated with his wisdom. He was killed during the Aesir-Vanir war (when two factions of Norse gods fought), but Odin enchanted his head to stay alive and assist him. I stuck to that part of the myth, but the rest was my own invention. Mímir never built himself a creepy body of old animal parts and he never kidnapped Idun, goddess of the apples of immortality.

Idun was captured, however, and it was from this myth that I borrowed much of Bree's challenge. The "son of a suitor of Greip" was an actual kenning (Norse poetic turn of phrase) that was used in the story about Idun's kidnapping. It did actually refer to a giant, in this case Thjazi. Idun was eventually rescued by the gods and Thjazi killed for his transgressions. I changed the story to give it the twist of Mímir conducting the kidnapping, though he never did in the real stories.

Another Norse story that I borrowed from was the tale of Utgard-Loki and his challenges. I wanted to send Bree on a true Norse hero's journey, and this was the perfect one. There are two contradictory versions of the tale, but Thor and Loki feature in both. As does the Jotunn, Utgard-Loki (who in some versions in Loki himself). The famous Icelandic scribe Snorri Sturluson recorded one version of this tale. The purpose of this tale was entertainment, and the elements were as ridiculous as I portrayed them to be.

It's a much longer tale than what I told, and I twisted it around a bit. The riddle that Mímir asked Bree to solve is actually from this story—the one in which Loki and Logi the fire god battle it out to see who can eat fastest. Logi wins, of course.

The race against thought, Hugi, was conducted by Thjalfi, a very fast member of Thor's party. Hugi obviously won. It was Thor who attempted to lift the cat, and also Thor who was required to battle the old woman, who he later learned represented old age. The twist in *Master of Magic* was that the cat was in a cat lady's house and the cat lady was old age. I wish I could say that this was my idea, but it came from my friend's thirteen year old son, Griffin. Zoe, ten years old, helped with other aspects of the story. It turned out to be my favorite part!

That's it for the mythological elements in *Master of Magic*. Hopefully I didn't miss any other historic elements. Thank you again for reading the books, and I hope you enjoyed Bree's adventure. Ana's will be coming up next!

ACKNOWLEDGMENTS

Thank you, Ben, for everything. There would be no books without you.

Thank you to Lindsey Loucks and Jena O'Connor for your excellent editing. The book is immensely better because of you! Thank you to Griffin and Zoe for your help with the trials at Yggdrasil. The cat lady and cat house were inspired.

Thank you to Orina Kafe for the beautiful cover art. Thank you to Collette Markwardt for allowing me to borrow the Pugs of Destruction, who are real dogs named Chaos, Havoc, and Ruckus. They were all adopted from rescue agencies.

GLOSSARY

Alpha Council - There are two governments that enforce law for supernaturals—the Alpha Council and the Order of the Magica. The Alpha Council governs all shifters. They work cooperatively with the Alpha Council when necessary—for example, when capturing FireSouls.

Blood Sorcerer - A type of Magica who can create magic using blood.

Dark Magic - The kind that is meant to harm. It's not necessarily bad, but it often is.

Demons - Often employed to do evil. They live in various hells but can be released upon the earth if you know how to get to them and then get them out. If they are killed on Earth, they are sent back to their hell.

Dragon Sense - A FireSoul's ability to find treasure. It is an internal sense that pulls them toward what they seek. It is easiest to find gold, but they can find anything or anyone that is valued by someone.

Djinn - Possesses invisibility and the ability to possess others for brief periods of time.

Earthwalking Gods - Reincarnates of the ancient gods who

can walk upon the earth. They are mortal but with all the power of that god.

Eclektica - A jack-of-all-trades who deals in spells.

Enchanted Artifacts – Artifacts can be imbued with magic that lasts after the death of the person who put the magic into the artifact (unlike a spell that has not been put into an artifact—these spells disappear after the Magica's death). But magic is not stable. After a period of time—hundreds or thousands of years depending on the circumstance—the magic will degrade. Eventually, it can go bad and cause many problems.

Fire Mage – A mage who can control fire.

FireSoul - A very rare type of Magica who shares a piece of the dragon's soul. They can locate treasure and steal the gifts (powers) of other supernaturals. With practice, they can manipulate the gifts they steal, becoming the strongest of that gift. They are despised and feared. If they are caught, they are thrown in the Prison of Magical Deviants.

The Great Peace - The most powerful piece of magic ever created. It hides magic from the eyes of humans.

Magica - Any supernatural who has the power to create magic—witches, sorcerers, mages. All are governed by the Order of the Magica.

Order of the Magica - There are two governments that enforce law for supernaturals—the Alpha Council and the Order of the Magica. The Order of the Magica govern all Magica. They work cooperatively with the Alpha Council when necessary—for example, when capturing FireSouls.

Seeker - A type of supernatural who can find things. FireSouls often pass off their dragon sense as Seeker power.

Seklie - Sea creatures lived off the coasts of Ireland and Scotland. They are seals who can also become human and draw their magic from the sea.

Shifter - A supernatural who can turn into an animal. All are governed by the Alpha Council.

Transporter - A type of supernatural who can travel anywhere. Their power is limited and must regenerate after each use.

Undercover Protectorate - A secret organization dedicated to protecting supernaturals and solving the crimes that no one else will.

Vampire - Blood drinking supernaturals with great strength and speed who live in a separate realm.

ABOUT LINSEY

Before becoming a writer, Linsey Hall was a nautical archaeologist who studied shipwrecks from Hawaii and the Yukon to the UK and the Mediterranean. She credits fantasy and historical romances with her love of history and her career as an archaeologist. After a decade of tromping around the globe in search of old bits of stuff that people left lying about, she settled down and started penning her own romance novels. Her Dragon's Gift series draws upon her love of history and the paranormal elements that she can't help but include.

COPYRIGHT

Copyright 2018 by Linsey Hall
Published by Bonnie Doon Press LLC

Linsey@LinseyHall.com
www.LinseyHall.com
https://www.facebook.com/LinseyHallAuthor
ISBN 978-1-942085-57-7